THE STORY

Val Edward Simone

A Morningside Publishing Book
Payson, Arizona

THE STORY

A Morningside Publishing, LLC Book

Text Copyright © 2015 by Val Edward Simone
Revised Text Copyright © 2019 by Val Edward Simone
All Rights Reserved.

Printed in the United States of America

Library of Congress Control Number: 2015901511

Printed Version
ISBN 978-1-936210-59-6

Cover Design: Val Edward Simone

For more books please visit:
www.morningsidepublishing.com
www.ekidslandpublishing.com

MORNINGSIDE
PUBLISHING, LLC
PAYSON, ARIZONA

Dedication:
To every one of us who love stories with our Jack

With Special Thanks To:
Editor
Rita Samols

Musical Inspiration
Secret Garden

For Consideration:

"When it is that the created becomes the Creator,
then shall it be also when the slave rises above the Master!"
~ **The Story**

CHAPTER 1

I walked into the bar. It was dark. It was like stepping into a tomb. Smelled like a tomb. Hell, it was a tomb, I guess, for all those lost souls lined up along the bar staring down into their drinks, praying for death to come and free them. They looked dead already. The mortician behind the bar glanced up at me. "Double Jack, neat," I said. He nodded without smiling. He was used to dealing with the dead.

She sat at the end of death row. She was alone. From a distance she looked pretty good. But then, they always look good from a distance.

I guessed her to be about twenty-five, with blonde hair settled down lazily over the shoulders of a little black dress. Long, hanging earrings sparkled even in the dim light. They were probably zirconium. Most drunks usually hock the good stuff for booze money, but she looked sexy as hell. So why was she alone? Did I really care to know? If they're alone, looking like that, there's usually a pretty good reason. Why tempt fate? Why start something I'd only regret later?

Damn. There was only one stool open. It was next to her. Just my luck. The kind of luck I don't need. I thought about it. Hell, I concluded, I was dead anyway, like all these other corpses. What more harm could it do?

What a dumb question. What more harm could it do? You idiot. It could do a lot more harm. She could want to talk, open up to me and tell me all her troubles. Christ! I don't need that. I didn't come here to play lonely hearts games. I came here to drink. I came here to forget my own troubles. Why the hell would I want to hear about hers?

I saw her up close. Jesus! She's hot! She must be pretty messed up in the head. I sat down.

My drink arrived. "Open a tab," I said.

"You got the money?" asked the mortician.

I reached into my pocket and pulled out a wad of cash.

"Tab's open, pal." The embalmer walked away.

Out of the corner of my eye I noticed her glass was just about empty. I asked myself, should I offer to buy her a drink? NO! Damn it all, you fool. She'll want to talk.

That's how bad things begin, you know? First you talk, then you screw. Then someone dies. I didn't feel like dying today. I didn't feel like killing either. I didn't even feel like screwing.

What's that they say, 'leave sleeping dogs alone' or some shit? Do it, fool! Leave the bitch alone.

"You wanna buy me a drink, but you're afraid I'll want to talk to you," she said.

I hated what she said. Actually, I hated the *way* she said it, with that sultry "I'm going to kill you" voice. I hate that kind of voice. Draws me in every time. That's what happens to saps like me. They get drawn in — drawn in deep — deep into the mayhem and craziness. And shit like that usually ends in murder.

How did she do that? She some kind of mind reader? Now I know why she's alone. Scares the hell out of guys who hate to have their secrets exposed.

"So, are ya?" I asked.

"No. I came here to drink, not talk."

Damn, I thought. She's getting hotter by the second.

"Good. In that case, I'll be glad to buy you a drink."

"Don't need you to. I'm rich as hell. I don't need anything from you."

Okay. Now I *really* know why she's alone — got a chip on her shoulder a mile wide.

"Works for me," I shot back. "I ain't looking for trouble anyway. Got enough of my own."

"Ain't we all?"

"Damn! We're talking."

She smirked.

"Damn! We are at that."

"How the hell did that happen?" I asked, amused and confused.

She smirked again. "Hell if I know."

"So what do we do now?"

"We might as well screw each other's brains out."

"Damn!"

"Yeah. Damn!"

At that moment I knew this evening was going to end bloody — very bloody. The only question in my mind was whose blood it was going to —

BEEEEEEEEEEEEP!

The microwave notified me that my lunch was ready. I pushed myself away from my laptop and my latest attempt at writing my next book.

That's how it was in my house. That's how it always was in my house — the house of Vincent Hobbs, number one best-selling author. If my dinner didn't BEEP, I didn't eat. That's a lie. To be truthful, if my *real* dinner didn't go SPLUNKCLUNK, I wouldn't eat, drink, or whatever the hell that's supposed to mean. Oh, by the way, the splunkclunk is the sound ice cubes make when they splash into a highball glass filled with liquid love. That would be Jack Daniel's Tennessee whiskey — the true inspiration of my life lately.

So why is this important? It's not. But then much in my life at that time wasn't important. I'll tell you this, though. If I'd known I had only a few days to live, I'd have done things differently. What am I saying? That's bullshit. I'd probably live my last days exactly the same way. Hell, I wouldn't change a thing. That's the kind of fool I am. But perhaps I'm getting ahead of myself.

That particular day began like many others had over the last several months, with the early morning phone call from my agent, Arnie Feinstein, reminding me that his presentation to the publishers was set for the following Monday, exactly one week away, and I'd better have my synopsis completed very soon.

I was in a bit of hot water with my agent. I was supposed to have the synopsis for my latest book to him last month so he could present it to the group of publishers he was planning on submitting the project to. Problem was, I was fresh out of new ideas. Well, that's only one of many problems I had since I took to strong drink. Hell. Okay. I'll be honest with you. I had been spending most of my time fully in the bag for the last year.

Yeah. I had issues then. So who hasn't? But mine were apparently keeping me from satisfying my commitments to my agent. I'm a hot author, it seems. I've had four number one best sellers in the last four years. My books are still selling by the millions. My publisher, a hotshot by the name of Randall James, is making a lot of money and he wants to strike while my iron is hot, so to speak.

But what he didn't yet know was that my iron had cooled about a month before the publication of my latest book. That was seven months ago and it didn't look like it was about to heat up anytime soon. I didn't have a clue what I should or could write.

My buddy Jack soothed me, though. He understood the many pressures I was under. He sympathized with me about how tough it was to keep pumping out number one best sellers. The publishing world is tough enough. Being number one is like having a target on your back. Everyone is taking shots at you, hoping to dethrone you and take over your sweet spot on top of the heap, above the crap they're putting out thinking it's great material. What boobs they are.

It's hell being at the top, but my publisher didn't want to hear about my troubles. He just wanted the next book — four months ago.

Jack had been helping me get through my *sorrowful days*. That's what I called them, although they weren't really sorrowful. Hell's bells, I still can't remember most of them, and what I do recall were mostly good times.

Of course, there was that incident last summer when I got with nature, you might say, and ran naked through the woods and scared the crap out of those two women hikers. I suppose Jack had something to do with it. But it ended okay, as I recall. Jack reached out to them in a friendly gesture and we all ended up naked and frolicking in a nearby river. So, thinking back on my sorrowful days, I can't say there had been too much sorrow in my life. But then there was my agent.

I have nothing against agents. In my line of work they're a necessary evil, and Arnie's been good for me. So I was sitting there feeling bad that I had nothing to give him to present to the publishers. What can I say? I was a sorry sort.

In former moments, long-ago moments when sobriety returned during fleeting early morning periods of wakefulness, I understood that my failure to produce the synopsis was about to cost me at least eight hundred fifty large ones.

For those of you who lack understanding, that's eight hundred fifty thousand dollars. That was supposed to be my net advance on my next novel. Of course, to be honest, I didn't believe Arnie was worried about *my* money, but *his*. That was to be his hundred fifty thousand dollars from my million-dollar advance — his fifteen percent — his blood money. *Damn agents! Damn bloodsuckers!* Still, he did get me good deals. He'd helped make me rich. So I couldn't blame him for being nervous.

Nervous or not, I didn't have a thing for him to present, except maybe the opening lines I had just written to another psycho-lady-killer story. I had done that to death, though, and I didn't know how long I could continue to run with that theme.

My last three novels had the lady killer deeply involved. But I had killed her off in the last book. Damn, that felt good. The publishers, however, were wanting me to resurrect her. There's a saying in the fiction world: "No one stays dead forever if the money's right."

It's been my publisher's belief that the market hasn't had its fill yet of my sexy-looking nymphomaniac psycho killer. That's how publishers are. They want to bleed every drop out of a theme before dumping it. Actually, they want to drain every good book idea out of us authors before they dump *us*. It's only about the money. It's always about the money. *Damn publishers! Damn agents!*

Still, it made sense in a way, but I didn't have another story about her in me. I'd had enough of the psycho-killer genre. I was spent. I wanted to write about something else. I had a good opening going. I mean, everyone loves a guy-walking-into-a-bar opening, and if done correctly, the story could have gone anywhere from there.

But Randall James was expecting the story to go where it had always gone before — to the psycho bitch killer.

I had a problem with that. You see, I love women. I really do. And before I hit the bottle hard, I used to get along with them very well. I'm not so hot with them today. I think the Jack Daniel's thing had a hand in turning them off, but hey, I was a burgeoning alcoholic and that was just the way it was going to go.

Well, that might not be totally true. Perhaps the drinking thing had interfered with the boinking thing. Okay, I admit it. I couldn't get it up, but I had issues. I had stresses. I had real-world worries.

Of course all those excuses were bullshit. The truth was I was too drunk most of the time for sex. But all that didn't matter. Carla had left me long before the drinking ever really took hold of me.

Something about me not being there for her emotionally.

"Hell," I said, "I'm emotional. I cry watching *Old Yeller*."

"It's not the same," she said and then she smacked me between the running lights.

Picking myself up off the floor, grinning like a fool, tasting the blood in my mouth, I realized what she was talking about. She had difficulty getting a rise outa me. Not that kind. The other kind. The kind that led to emotional rage — to violent actions. She loved violence. I didn't. I think that's what truly got her off. She loved getting smacked around. She was a mongoose, I was a dove. It wasn't working out well. That is, until one day seven months ago. When it got worse.

I had had a few drinks. I was feeling giddy. Carla was standing right in front of me chatting away about something boring and uninspiring. I smacked her in the kisser for no other reason than she was within reach. It felt good. A bit odd, but strangely good, therapeutic even. But she slugged me back with a whopping right cross that sent me ass over elbows onto the hard wood floor of my house. Damn, I thought, the welt blossoming next to my left eye, I really love this chick. She helped me to my feet and then smacked me again. I hit the floor totally lost in love. Perhaps I have some kind of mental problem.

I'm not sure anymore. I guess I won't ever know what mysterious power she held over me. After she smacked the crap outa me, she left. I haven't seen her since. Maybe I had it all wrong. Maybe she only liked doing the smacking, not getting smacked. I don't really know. I stopped wondering. I had Jack to comfort me, so I didn't really care that she left. Maybe I didn't care that she'd ever been there.

CHAPTER 2

For the last ten years I had lived just outside the small mid-Rockies town of Alma, Colorado. Actually, I lived about five miles up winding dirt roads in the mountains above Alma in a modern log house set into a south-facing slope on the east end of a heavily treed forty-acre parcel of land. It was perfect for me and pretty isolated.

In the past, on warm sunny days, I tossed my laptop into my truck and drove five additional miles up more rutty dirt roads to a high-altitude lake named Lake Elizabeth. It was a naturally formed lake in the heart of a granite mountain called Zeke's Peak. With my legs dangling over the edge of a 300-foot cliff, I had done some of my best writing.

I used to find it peaceful and inspiring to sit there and stare out over the lake, allowing my mind to wander where it pleased.

Things changed, though. After Carla left, I didn't seem to find anything inspiring or peaceful.

I suspected that I had succumbed to what can be called the *Jack Daniel's Consequence*, or, as it was most commonly referred to within *my* circle of drunks, the *JD Effect*. Alcoholics tend to be morose and depressed most of the time — inclined to seeing darkness rather than light. And any setback, no matter what the level of its severity, is usually viewed with defeating skepticism. But I found it hard to blame all my maladies on Brother Jack. Besides, Carla *was* a crazy bitch. I concluded that I was better off without her around. But the woes of depression are an ever-present nemesis to be dealt with, and I didn't deal with the woes very well.

There was another bit of a downside to being a minimally functioning alcoholic living a hermit's life up in the mountains far away from civilization. I mean besides having to battle depression and my own wild alcohol-induced hallucinations from time to time, there was the mornings-after afflictions, we'll call them, following the nights of binging that brought me some of my most difficult realities concerning my ever-worsening condition.

Take one morning about a month ago, for instance. I woke up with my tongue glued to the dusty wood floor by dried saliva and had to pee really bad. I thought about crawling to the toilet, but that was all the way across the room, much too far for a man who didn't yet have full control of his legs, senses, or bladder, as well as having a mouth full of lint. The gas fireplace was closer.

Thinking back on it now, I probably should have turned off the flame first, but I didn't. I didn't even think about it. The next thing I recognized, barely, was the boiled-piss vapor rolling up out of the flames and forming a cloud over my head. It was about to rain piss, but it was too late to change tactics. I was in full stream.

Carla walked out of the bedroom. Damn, I thought, I don't remember her coming back.

"You've got to be kidding me," she said.

I realized then that she was just one of my many realistic hallucinations.

I ignored her. She disappeared. But there I was, pissing on a gas-fed fire. I knew at that moment my new day wasn't going to be any better than the day before, or the day before that. And considering how much Jack I had drunk the previous night, I was also surprised that I wasn't pissing a line of flame into the fireplace. I mean, it just had to be 90 percent alcohol.

"You need to back off on the drinking a bit," someone shouted.

"Who said that?" I shouted back.

Damn! It was me.

I discovered an almost empty bottle of morning sustenance lying on the floor near my computer table. After finishing my morning piss, I walked or crawled, I don't remember which, over to it and sucked the last of the nectar into my throat. It revived me.

I do remember dropping into my chair and staring at the lines I had written the night before about the guy walking into the bar. Unfortunately, that was all I had written.

I immediately wrote several more sentences, but they were crap. I had lost inspiration, and being Jackless for the moment, I didn't see inspiration returning anytime soon. She can really be a bitch sometimes; inspiration, that is. That's what I called my muse — Inspiration. Of course that was when I was being kind. Most of the last several months, I'd called her slut, whore, and other not-so-niceties. Actually, of late, I think she had been as drunk as I was and completely useless.

Still, I was momentarily excited. "That's a great opening though," I said. "A guy walks into a bar. I could take this somewhere, but where should I take it?"

Don't be alarmed. I usually carried on complete conversations with myself out loud. Most of the time I was the only one listening anyway.

A new thought spanked me. I like spankings, but I digress. I had had enough of psycho lady. I was certain of that. And from this opening bar scene I had the new idea that it could perhaps flow nicely into a really great love story.

So I silently stared at the screen for a moment until a spasm shook my body and I couldn't handle it any longer.

I got up from my chair and walked to a free-standing closet, opened the door, and smiled upon seeing twenty-five bottles of Jack Daniel's staring back at me. I pulled one from the shelf, twisted the top off, and took a big swallow.

My spasm departed.

I returned to my chair, highlighted everything I had written and dangled my index figure over the delete key. "Eat the bar scene. Bite the psycho bitch.

Enough corpses," I said and dropped my finger onto the key. The words disappeared.

I began to type the following words.

> She sat alone at the table along the wall of the restaurant, by the windows, looking like a million bucks. The moment I saw her, I fell in love. I guessed her to be about twenty-five, with blonde hair lazily settled down over her shoulders. She wore a short, strapless black dress. Long, dangling diamond earrings sparkled even in the dim light. I walked past her, she looked up. Our eyes met. I stopped.
>
> "Would you marry me?" I asked.
>
> "Could we get a bite to eat first? I'm starving."
>
> "That works for me," I said.
>
> "Would you like to join me?" she cooed. "I don't like eating alone."
>
> "NO!"

Wait! I stopped typing. That was weird. I didn't type that. I hit the backspace button several times, deleting "NO!" and then typed "Yes!" and hit the 'enter' key. "NO!" appeared on the screen. What the hell? I deleted it again, retyped "Yes!" and pressed the 'enter' key again. I blinked. "NO!" appeared again.

I reached for the bottle, raised it up to my mouth, and took a giant swallow.

"What's going on?" I mumbled. I repeated each step once more and pressed the 'enter' key. The screen displayed "NO!"

"Son of a —" I repeated each step a final time and pressed the 'enter' key. The screen still read "NO!"

"Okay, fine. Have it your way for now," I shouted. *"Damn contraption!"* I typed out another sentence.

"I sat down. We ate. We fell in love."

I pressed the 'enter' key. The screen read "I sat down. She knew at that very moment exactly how she was going to kill me."

What the hell? *Damn computers! Damn technology! Damn publishers! Damn agents!* I pushed away from the laptop and shut the lid. "I'm tired. I'll deal with you later," I said. "Stupid computer."

I grabbed my bottle. I walked to the front door. I opened it and stepped out onto the deck and plopped into a chair. It wasn't warm, but it wasn't cold either. It was an early fall Colorado morning.

I tried to make myself believe I was going to think about the book, but I lied to myself. I did that quite frequently. I twisted off the cap and tossed it away. I wouldn't need it again. Funny how sure I was about that when I wasn't sure about anything else in my life at that moment.

I took three big swallows. Each burned wonderfully down my throat. "I guess you're finished with writing today?" someone asked.

I turned to see who had said that. No one was there. "Jesus Christ," I said to myself. "You have got to get a handle on this talking-to-yourself crap."

"I say, I guess you're finished with writing today?" the voice asked again.

I got up off the chair and looked over the railing of the deck. It wasn't my imagination. It was Sheriff Dell Overly, sheriff of Park County, walking from his car toward the steps.

"Good morning, Dell," I shouted. "I'm glad it's you. I thought I was hearing voices again."

"That might have something to do with that bottle in your hand, I reckon."

"Quite possibly. I'm glad you're here for another reason, Dell. I want to show you something."

He walked up the steps and onto the deck. We shook hands and went into the house.

"You're not going to believe this," I stated with assurance.

"Okay. What ya got, Vincent?"

I opened my laptop. The computer had gone into sleep mode and the screen was blank. I pressed the space bar, reactivating it. The screen brightened.

On it was exactly what I had written before. I saw the word "Yes!" staring back at me.

"This ain't right," I insisted.

"What ain't right?"

Then I noticed the other words. "I sat down. We ate. We fell in love."

"That can't be right. I swear there were other words on the screen before."

"What are you talking about, Vincent?"

I quickly explained what had happened that morning when I'd tried to write. During the early part of my recitation, he looked at me earnestly, trying to understand. During the latter part of my story, he stared at me through eyes searching for the point of the joke I must be pulling on him.

He laughed at the end. "That was a good one, Vincent. The Jack hasn't dulled your creativity or sense of humor, I'll say that for ya."

I squinted at him through light-sensitive eyes. The morning sun had finally risen above the trees and was shining directly into my face. I raised a hand to shield the sun. "Dell, you don't understand. I wasn't trying to play a joke on you. What I told you really happened. Isn't that strange?"

He raised a hand to his face and pinched his nose. "What I find strange," he said, "is how it smells like piss in here."

"Oh yeah," I said. "About that. I pissed on the gas fireplace this morning. I was a little out of it. Sorry."

He fanned away the stench from his nose and shook his head.

"Boy, you gotta get a better handle on this drinking. It's getting the best of you, I believe."

"Yeah, Dell. You're exactly right about that." I unconsciously lifted the bottle to my mouth and took a long swig. I brought it down to my side absent any thought to the action. "I gotta get a grip on it for sure." Then I realized what I had just done. I grinned and shrugged my shoulders.

Dell just shook his head.

"At least you got sense enough not to try and drive sloshed."

"To tell you the truth, Dell, my battery died about a month ago and I haven't got a battery charger. I've been meaning to call you about it, but I keep forgetting."

"I believe that. I've got one at home. I'll bring it by as soon as I can."

"Thanks. I appreciate it. By the way, what brings you all the way up here today?"

"Just checking up on you. No one's heard from you in quite a spell down in Alma. I stopped in for a soda earlier at Joe Thompson's store. Joe asked me if I might come up and take a peek. They were all wondering if you were lying up here dead and rotting." He chuckled. "Come to think of it, smells like rotting death up here. But I'll tell everyone you're okay."

"They were probably hoping I *was* dead."

"Now, why would you go and say something like that, Vincent? Everyone loves you around here. You're our shining star. We've got a by golly bonafide celebrity right here in Park County. And, of course, let's not forget them two lovely hiker ladies who have taken a sure fancy to you down in Fairplay. Yes sir, they speak right well of you." He chuckled again.

He had an infectious laugh. I hated it. It made me happy and I didn't want to be happy at that moment. I'd have to kill him someday for it. In a story, that is.

"Yeah, well, give them all my best, Dell. Can you stay awhile and visit? It's been a bit too quiet up here lately. I think I'm losing it."

"I'd like to, Vincent, but I've got a meeting to go to in about an hour. How about another time?"

"Okay. Another time, then."

"Try easing up on the booze, Vince. That might help with the melancholy."

"I'll sure try."

I walked Dell out the door and to the steps.

"I'd better stop here, Dell. Once down those steps, I don't think I could make it back up here."

"Okay, Vincent. But seriously, you might wanna curb that drinking a bit. You're not looking in top form."

"I shall endeavor to try, Dell." I took another unconscious long swig before I caught myself again. I blame Dell for that. I was doing fine until he mentioned drinking. I guess I might have been on the impressionable side because of my delicate condition.

Dell drove away with a wave back to me from his window. I waved back and suddenly realized that I was still holding the bottle in my hand. I took another drink.

Then, like a burr under a horse's saddle, something bothered me. I went back to my computer and stared at the screen. All the right words were there. None of the contrary words were anywhere on the screen.

"Stupid computer!" I shouted.

CHAPTER 3

I sat on the sofa watching a late-morning reality TV show. Well, to be honest, the TV was on, but I wasn't watching. My mind was busy formulating the plot of my new book.

I realized that I had to accomplish something on the story line that day. If I knew Arnie as well as I thought I did, he'd be calling soon to remind me that I had less than a week to give him what he needed to make his pitch.

Because I had fulfilled the commitments of my previous contract and this was going to be a new multi-book agreement, he was hoping to start a bidding war between Randall James and two or three of the other big publishing firms that would substantially increase the advance — and his bloodsucking fee, of course.

He needed something strong and sure to pitch to them. Under those conditions, he was like a woodpecker drumming on me about it, every day calling "just to remind you of our commitment to the publishing process."

I heard four very loud beeps. They brought my mind back from wandering about on Plot Island. I called it *Plot Island* because when I worked on the plot of a book, I felt like I was marooned on a desert island and the only way back to civilization was to complete the plot. The plot was my only ticket off that damned island.

Hey, I realized, I still held a bottle of *plot elixir* in my hand. I took a long swallow. Nothing came to me. I took another long swallow just for the hell of it.

My stomach gurgled. I needed to eat something. Yeah, even alkies like me needed real food now and then. If I was correct, I had a cupboard full of Pop Tarts waiting for me.

I had a sudden thought about that. Strawberry Pop Tarts and Jack Daniel's. How about shortening that to *Pop Daniel's*? Nah, that sounded too much like a Walter Brennan character from some old forgotten Western. I know, how about *Jack Tarts*. Now that had real possibilities.

I decided I'd work on another version later. For now, I tore the packet open and plopped the two sweet doughy morsels into the toaster and pressed down the switch.

While I waited for the tarts to pop up, I took three or four good swigs of Jack. I was preparing my belly for the bombardment of bread and fruit. If I was my stomach, I reasoned, I wouldn't like to be surprised with anything, except with a splash of Jack, of course.

The second the toaster popped up my tarts, I heard four loud beeps again. I looked around. I was alone. I was hearing things. It was becoming a regular thing, but I wasn't yet used to the audio hallucinations that started about a month ago. I shook my head hard to clear my brain. It didn't work, but then I was starting to get used to a foggy brain.

I pulled the tarts from the toaster and dropped them onto a clean plate. I was surprised that I had a clean plate, but I did.

I chomped a few bites, followed by a Jack chaser. A *tart chaser*, I figured to call it. I don't know why I was so obsessed with naming things at that moment. But I was, so I flowed with it.

Four beeps broke into my thoughts. I became alert and listened. I farted. That was definitely a real sound; at least I thought it was. I farted again.

I was certain they weren't audio hallucinations. The beeps, that is. But in my condition I could have heard the voice of God calling out and not known it.

Four beeps once more. One more fart. Now more alert, I determined that they, the beeps, were coming from my computer. I stuffed the remaining tarts into my mouth, washed them down with a few swigs of Jack, and went to the computer.

Just before I got to it, BEEP! BEEP! BEEP! BEEP! ... FART!

I sat down at the computer and stared disbelievingly at the screen.

The contrary words were once again on the screen. I read them aloud. "*NO!*" and "*I sat down. She knew at that very moment exactly how she was going to kill me.*"

"What the hell is going on?" I said aloud. I looked at the bottle of the nearly drained Jack

Daniel's sitting majestically next to the computer — a silent sentinel to my remaining sanity.

"So what do you make of this, Jack?" I asked, hoping to hell the bottle wouldn't answer me. Thankfully, it remained silent.

Not to be outwitted by a computer, I highlighted all the wrong words and retyped them the way I wanted them to be. I wanted to write a love story. I had figured out that much, but I needed to work out the plotline. Not as much as I needed to in order to write the story, just a brief synopsis suitable for my agent to present to the publishers. I didn't need every detail worked out. In fact, I wouldn't want to do that. I generally used a synopsis more as a guide to writing the story, leaving the details to be worked out during the writing. I liked to give freedom to my creative intuition.

Still, I needed enough of an outline that Arnie could entice the publishers into parting with the large amount of money necessary to motivate me to write again. And since we were on the new ground of a new contract, I was hoping to break with the drivel of another psycho killer and stretch my creativity a bit. A love story would certainly do that, because, let's face it, I didn't have a clue what love was or how to write about it. It would be a wonderful change for me and a hell of a challenge. I was ready for a challenge.

Sure, it would be a tough task, but I was a professional, and a professional overcomes the limits of what he or she doesn't understand by doing research. If I could get the publisher to bite on the love angle, I'd delve headlong into the research phase immediately. I wanted to avoid the romance-novel theme at any cost. I reviled them. But a genuine love story, fraught with all its issues like suspected betrayal, yearning desire, tragic self-sacrifice, and desperate unfulfilled wishes, might be a fun project to undertake.

So there I sat, staring hopefully at the computer screen waiting for inspiration to strike. I could have sat there until hell froze over because I got nothing from the ether. Ether, the place where my muse lives — somewhere beyond time and space — the place where Inspiration hailed from. And although it might be a physically unreachable place, I'm certain it exists, because all of my novels had been born there, in her faraway, mystical land. They were good novels, too. But somewhere along the way, my muse must have either found a new protégé to inspire or had tumbled into her own bottle of Jack and had forgotten about me. But I've already mentioned that, so let's move on.

I'd barely had any ideas come to me since I had completed my last novel. That was well over a year ago. It was a short time later that I discovered the curative properties of Jack Daniel's for the oblivion created by lost creativity. Of course, along with the cure for some maladies, Jack might have created new ones, different ones. But I wasn't about to go blaming my problems on my buddy. No, sir.

I had been considering it only a queer coincidence that I'd been virtually without any thoughts as to how I was going to kick-start my next literary endeavor. But lately, I've begun to have my suspicions about my brooding, intoxicated, or absent muse.

I reached for the bottle. It was exactly where I had left it several minutes ago. I missed it. I picked it up and gave it a hug and then I drained it.

I should have given the empty a dignified burial. Instead, I stood up and walked to the closet, dropping the empty unceremoniously into the garbage can as I went. I drew another bottle from the closet, twisted the cap off, French-kissed the opening, and swallowed a good deal of the golden-brown liquid. I felt instantly better. Not that I felt bad before, but better now.

I returned to the computer a happy man. My happiness did not remain long, however.

As I sat down, the screen had changed once again. "*NO!*" and "*I sat down. She knew at that very moment exactly how she was going to kill me*" had returned.

"What the hell is going on?" I shouted my question, but no response came. I was almost glad for that.

I buried my head in my hands and wondered if I was going completely mad, which, strangely, isn't that far from being totally snockered. I heard a beep. I looked up at the screen. It read: **"DON'T YOU DARE TRY TO CHANGE THE PLOT AGAIN."**

Okay, I *knew* I didn't type that. At least I was pretty certain I hadn't. So how did it get on my screen? Someone or something had to have typed the sentence out. That was clear — as clear as it could be considering how inebriated I was at the moment.

No, I was certain. It couldn't have been me. I understood, even then, that alcoholics can never be certain about too much that goes on in their life except that they're alcoholics. But this had crossed the line. I've typed drunk before. Okay, most of the time lately, but I had never been so drunk that I didn't know if I was typing or not.

I stared at those words and wondered what was happening. I was then unexpectedly overcome with fear. Who or what had visited me in my house?

From the words of warning, such as they were, on the screen, I guessed it wasn't a friendly visit.

I remembered that when I bought the property, I noted no dreadful history connected to it. There had been no reports of any deaths occurring in the house or on the property. So there should be no reason for the presence of any angry spirit. In fact, I do recall that it was built and formerly owned by a very nice couple who had grown weary of the cold winters common to that part of Colorado and retired to Arizona. Therefore, there was nothing I knew of about this house or property that would warrant any abnormal concerns regarding an unruly ghostly presence.

Now that I had ruled out that kind of haunting, that left what? I didn't have a frickin' clue. I took a long tug on the bottle and set it back down on the table next to the laptop.

One thing was certain to me. Well, that's a lie, for as I stated earlier, alcoholics are never really certain of anything except that we need that next drink. Therefore, to clarify, one thing I strongly suspected, because I had no proof, was that the computer didn't type those words by itself. Someone had to type on keys, either here or remotely.

A hacker! Yeah! That had to be it. But then I felt stupid. I wasn't connected to the internet. I don't care how good a hacker is, or the NSA for that matter, no one can get to a computer that's not connected to the internet without some pretty sophisticated hardware. No, it was not a hack attack.

"Vincent," I finally said aloud, "you might have to face a cold, hard truth, buddy. You must have typed it out yourself. Perhaps you're more shit-faced than you think you are and you blacked out, typed the words, and came back."

No, I inwardly insisted. I *didn't* type those words.

"Then who did?" I heard myself ask out loud.

"I don't know."

"So if the computer didn't type them, and you didn't type them, who the hell did? Are you hearing yourself?"

I was, but at that point I didn't know who I was.

If that makes any sense to you, then you're one up on me.

"I know what it sounds like," I shouted, "but I'm telling you, I didn't type it!"

"It sounds like it could be a line from one of your books. Maybe it's just some old code showing up."

"In a complete sentence?" I asked myself.

"Maybe it was a line from one of your previous books that didn't get fully erased."

"No, it's not," I insisted. "I've never written a line like that before."

"Well, from what I know about these contraptions," I told myself, referring, of course, to my laptop, "they're fickle. Just erase the unwanted words and reboot the damned thing."

"I'm going to do just that. Right now," I replied to myself.

And that's exactly what I did.

The screen went blank.

CHAPTER 4

After the computer came back online and I had opened the document, I noticed that what I had written before and deleted was back: "*NO!*" and all the other contrary words, including "*She knew exactly how she was going to kill me.*"

I sat back in my chair and stared at the screen. "This makes no sense," I blurted out.

That wasn't a big revelation, even considering how pickled my brain was, but it was the only thing I could think of. In reality, though, it really *didn't* make any sense.

I got an idea into my head. I typed out "I'm the author." I pressed the 'enter' key. The sentence printed on the screen exactly as I had typed it.

"That's better," I said aloud. "It must have had a glitch that the reboot fixed. That was very strange."

I deleted the old story completely this time and retyped the synopsis of my new love story into the computer. In fact, I worked all day typing out the plot ideas that came to me without the glitch showing itself again.

I pushed back from the computer and looked at my wristwatch. It read 5:30 p.m. It was a good day's work for a slosher like me. It was going to be a good love story. I was happy with where it was heading, at least as a synopsis.

Arnie was expecting a synopsis of roughly forty to fifty pages. I had ten completed by the time I was ready to quit for the day. Of course, he wasn't expecting a love story, but screw him, I thought. I'm the author. I'll write what I damn well please.

Taking my bottle with me, I moved to the sofa and plopped down onto it, foolishly thinking that everything was going to work out just fine from here on. I had earned a well-deserved drink. I guzzled a good deal of the bottle. All was well again in the Vincent Hobbs home, I thought.

Boy, was I wrong, because that was about the time all hell broke loose.

* * * * *

I had fallen asleep on the sofa and was awakened by those four distinct beeps again.

I opened my eyes. I could barely keep them open. I guess I was more tired than I'd realized. The beeps sounded again.

"Oh, no," I mumbled.

I jumped up off the sofa and dashed over to the computer. I dropped into the chair. I gasped.

All my new words were gone and on the screen were newer words, printed as before, in a larger bold font and capitalized: **"YOU'VE BEEN WARNED!"**

In my shock, I deleted the words and then searched my hard drive. My new love synopsis was thankfully still intact on it. I pulled it up and breathed a relieved breath. "It's still here, thank goodness."

"Vincent. What's wrong with you?"

I looked up toward the voice, certain now that it was another audio hallucination. To my added shock, I was staring at a physical manifestation of my hallucinogenic mind.

"Carla? Is that really you? Are you truly here?"

"She walked over and smacked me across the face so hard I saw stars. She bent low and smiled.

"Did you feel that?"

"Yes. It hurt."

"Then it must be me and I must be here. Miss me?"

"Missed *you*. Didn't miss the smacking."

She raised her hand to smack me again. I cringed. She laughed.

"Coward."

"I'm a gentleman."

"I say you're a coward." She raised her hand again.

"Fine, I'm a coward. If it gets you to stop slapping me."

She lowered her hand, but only to take my bottle off the desk, lift it to her own mouth, and swallow several swigs.

She moved around behind me and read a few lines of the new story idea.

"Is this drivel going to be your next book?"

"Yeah. What's wrong with it?"

"It sucks. That's what's wrong with it? A love story? Really? You're actually attempting to write a love story?"

She laughed out loud. Howled was more like it. I knew she must have feral instincts hidden in her DNA somewhere, but I didn't know till then that she could actually howl.

"Why is that so funny? You don't think I can pull it off?"

"Hardly, Vinnie. You don't know anything about love."

"I can learn. I can research."

"You write about murder. That's been your success so far. Why venture into an area you know nothing about? Isn't it said that writers should write about what they know?"

I jumped up and grabbed the bottle out of her hand and nearly drank it dry. I sat back down. She grabbed it out of my hand and finished it.

"Look at that," she said. "I even have to finish your bottle for you. You're pathetic, you know that?"

"Why did you come back, then?"

"I had nothing better to do. Besides, I need some money."

"Ah. That explains it."

"Come on, Vincent. Do we always need to argue?"

"*I* don't need to. But it seems you do. It's like you're addicted to whatever thrill can be gotten from a good fight."

"Hmm, you might be right about that."

She bent over, I thought to kiss me on the cheek. Instead, she smacked the lights out of my skull. I tumbled out of my chair and hit the floor, seeing more than stars. I saw planets too — big ones, with rings like Saturn … and moons, lots of moons.

"What was *that* for?" I asked, trying to clear my head of the astronomical oddities.

"For not stopping me when I left you."

"Why would I try to stop you? It was *your* idea to go."

"You see now? You don't know the first thing about love. I wanted you to stop me from leaving. You were supposed to tell me how much you loved me and that you couldn't stand for me to leave. But you didn't. You just let me go without so much as a goodbye."

Okay. What she said was true enough. I did do that. I didn't try to stop her. But let me ask you this. Would you try to stop somebody from leaving after they just smacked the snot out of you? Yeah. I didn't think so.

"You just slapped me silly and left. I thought you wanted to leave."

"I wanted you to stop me. I wanted you to show me that you were capable of being some kind of a man. But you just sat on your ass on the floor and watched me leave."

"So you want me to now be happy that you came back so you could slap me around again? Do I have that right?"

I couldn't wait for her answer. I didn't think I was going to like it anyway. I picked myself up off the floor and went to the closet and retrieved another bottle.

"Wow!" she said. "You're really prepared."

"Prepared?"

"Yeah. For the long haul. You could stay drunk forever and avoid all your issues."

"I don't see why you should care about that."

"I'm back, butthead. I need you writing and making money, not drinking yourself to death. You dying an alcoholic's death does me no good."

"Thanks for your compassion." I twisted the top off the bottle and tossed it into the garbage can. You know the reason why.

"Don't start any shit with me, Vincent. I didn't come back here to listen to your pitiful excuses. Now sit your ass down and start writing a story you're capable of writing. And quit this love story bullshit. You'd never pull it off anyway. You know nothing about a loving relationship."

"Maybe not," I answered, refusing to sit down. "But I'm done with psycho bitches."

"Is that directed at me?"

She approached me and raised her hand to strike.

"No!" I said, cringing. "I just meant —"

"I don't care what you meant. Sit your ass down and write me a Vincent Hobbs novel that the world expects a Vincent Hobbs novel to be."

She motioned for me to sit. I stood still. She raised her hand, threatening to strike me again. I sat down, having no desire to take another trip through the solar system.

"Now delete this crap and give me murder, mayhem, and psycho chicks out of control."

"I can do that by taking notes right now."

She smacked me up the back side of my head. I saw the hint of Saturn forming before my eyes.

"Don't get smart with me, buster, or I'll really start smacking you around."

I know this is going to sound sickly strange, but I was glad she was back. She was giving me the direction I needed, the focus and inspiration I lacked. I got excited. Hell, I got an erection!

Then she smacked me across the face for staring at her tits.

"You'll get the candy after you've earned it and not before." She really smacked me again. Say hello to the stars, moons, and planets. But I lost my erection.

I started typing the original opening. "I walked through the door."

She shanghaied my bottle off the table. "And you'll get this after you've earned it, too."

Something snapped in my head.

I jumped up, snatched my bottle back, and then punched her so hard she went flying across the room and landed on the wood floor and skidded up against the closet full of Jack Daniel's. Fear suddenly gripped me tightly. Did I break any bottles?

I moved toward the closet, setting my bottle down on the computer table as I approached my stash. Carla lay sprawled out on the floor, going in and out of consciousness. I didn't care about her. I reached over her prone body for the closet handle.

"Don't you ever touch my Jack again, bitch!" I bellowed.

I tried to open the closet. Her body blocked the doors. I harshly tugged her out of the way and thrust the doors open, holding my breath. All the remaining bottles were intact. I breathed again, shut the door, and walked away, leaving her crumpled up on the floor, moaning.

Her moaning stopped abruptly. She jumped up and hit me hard in the back. It forced the breath out of my lungs. I tumbled hard to the floor, barely able to breathe.

She growled at me. Yes, you heard me right. She actually growled.

I looked up at her. Her eyes were turning bright yellow.

"You write that original story or I'll kill you," she threatened in a deep, gravelly voice. It wasn't her voice but that of some unknown beast.

She started to shake violently. I was mysteriously and curiously mesmerized by her trembling, her tits bouncing wildly around under her blouse. I was getting another erection.

The fascination did not last long, however, and neither did my woody, for as I stared at her, long black hairs began growing out of her face. So many that they eventually formed a full beard. Large white fangs then formed in the corners of her mouth. Seconds later, I could barely see her face at all. Just those bright yellow eyes staring at me and her fangs now dripping with viscous saliva. I gazed up at her with wide eyes and a mouth hung open in stupefied disbelief.

She grew upward until her five-foot-four, 100-pound frame became a six-foot-five, 275-pound hulk of seething rage. Her sudden growth shredded her clothing.

Her hands grew into paws with razor-sharp claws. She grew black hair all over her body, then her face transformed into the snarling, saliva-dripping snout of a vicious wolf. This could not be possible. My ex-girlfriend was transforming into a terrifying werewolf.

Seconds later, what stood before me was the horrific vision of what I considered to be my very end.

I jumped to my feet. I needed a slug of Jack. I needed it bad, but I realized, in that horrid moment, that my hands were empty. Where the hell was my beloved Jack? Had my courage departed willfully from me? Had it disavowed my very existence?

There I stood, facing this horrible creature and, with no way of summoning a fortifying courage, I stood worse than naked. I was scared and alone and becoming sober.

"Carla," I finally said, employing the last vestiges of whatever I might have called courage left within me. "Okay. I get it. You're a bit pissed. I understand that. Maybe I could work the original plotline into the love story and then end it as a romantic tragedy. How about that?"

I received only a guttural snarl from the beast. Then, to my astonishment, she attacked.

The Carla werewolf came at me. I wondered, in only an instant, how many other drunken authors had ever faced a werewolf. The Jack Daniel's bottle seemed a lifetime away, on my computer table. And the damned werewolf was between me and the computer table and my treasured Jack.

A sharp realization set in on me. If I wanted it, I would have to kill the werewolf. If I'd had my Jack bottle, I'd have hit the bitch right across her jaw. But Jack was on the other side of the room. So I decided right then and there that I'd have to kick the werewolf's ass if for no other reason than she stood between me and my buddy.

The first contact was not to my advantage. She struck me in the chest with her mighty right paw. The force of it sent me flying across the room. I landed at the base of the fireplace with a thunderous crash, spilling the fireplace tools. My mind tried to form any kind of thought, but it only responded from a primitive instinct for survival.

I rose up snarling myself. All thought of reason and compassion left me. I wanted my sip of Jack. And that became my sole motivation to engage this terrible beast.

I then recalled the sterling silver candelabra on the mantel that my mother had given me on my last birthday, "to light your way when life becomes too dark." My mother was like that. She was a metaphysical being in human form. Right now, however, she shone like a savior to me. Maybe she had known something I hadn't.

I snatched it from the mantel at the same moment Carla came at me, with dripping fangs and extended claws positioned to tear the flesh from my body.

I spun around at the last second and drove the candelabra deep into the creature's chest. The silver reacted immediately, not only halting the beast's attack but also sending it backward, howling horrifically. I had to cover my ears, for the shriek was so sharp and deafening I thought it capable of splitting my head into halves.

The werewolf fell onto its back and clutched at the silver candelabra with both hands, or paws, attempting to pull it from its chest. But I had buried it deep, and the mortally wounded beast, the silver doing its magic, did not have the strength to wrench it from its body. It howled mournfully, its paws smoldering from their contact with the sterling silver.

It cried out in desperation as I stepped over it, dashed to the computer table, and snatched up the bottle containing the rest of my courage. I swallowed the brown liquid gratefully.

I pulled the bottle from my lips and blew a relieved breath into the air, not caring about the beast, in terrific anguish, writhing on the floor behind me. I cared only that I once again held the sacred bottle in my grasp.

I turned around and stared at the thrashing beast on the floor. It was dying, but no morsel of compassion found its way into my hardened heart.

Armed now with Jack's courage, I walked over to the dying creature and stared down at it, filled with unwavering resolve. "I've changed my mind, Carla. I'm going to write a love story. But it won't be about *you*, bitch!"

I raised my right foot high over the howling beast. "I ain't missing you at all."

I slammed my foot down onto the end of the candelabra, driving it deeper into the beast's chest. The beast stilled. It died. I took another long swig of whiskey. The frightful ordeal was over.

I walked to the computer table and sat down in my chair. I stared at the computer screen. I thought for a few seconds and then began to type, speaking the words aloud as I wrote: "This is *my* story. I am the sole author. I'll write it any damn way I want. And there isn't anything you can do about it." I pressed the 'enter' key. The words appeared on the screen just as I had typed them. Victory was mine!

CHAPTER 5

The next day began as most others did, I'm afraid. I woke up sprawled out on the hard wood floor where I had passed out the night before after my victory celebration.

Picking my head up, I looked around. To my astonishment, the house was undisturbed. Furthermore, the body of the expired werewolf was absent as well. I figured it out.

"Damn!" I shouted and rose up off the floor to my knees. "It was all just another alcohol-induced hallucination."

My eyes wandered up to the mantel. The candelabra was there just as it had been before.

"I've got to get a handle on this drinking thing," I mumbled.

Those words inspired me. I jumped to my feet and looked around the room in a near panic. I calmed when I saw my half-full bottle of Jack on the end table next to the sofa.

I picked it up and swallowed as much as I could stand. Perhaps *inspired* is not the correct word to use to describe my reaction. Nevertheless, the result of such motivation resulted in me rebalancing my sense of self. I took another swallow to reassure myself of my regained emotional and mental stability.

The phone rang. I answered.

"Hello, Arnie," I said knowingly.

"How did you know it was me, Vincent?"

"Just a guess."

"Well, tell me, kid. How are you doing?"

"I'm well, thank you. Although I'm having weird halluci—"

"I meant on the plot synopsis."

"Oh, that. I'm getting to it. It's coming. Hey, it's gonna be a great love story."

"Love story? What the hell are you talking about? It's supposed to be a murder mystery."

"I changed my mind. I'm writing a love story."

"To hell with that, Vincent! I can't sell a damn love story. Besides, what the hell do you know about love? Write what you know, Vincent! And you know murder."

I hit the speaker switch and collapsed onto the sofa, cradling my bottle.

"But I don't want to write about murder anymore, Arnie. I want to write about something else."

"I've got three of the biggest publishers ready to cough up about two million five hundred thousand for another Vincent Hobbs murder mystery. They're champing at the bit for another psycho-lady killer novel. There's going to be a bidding battle like you can't believe. I can't change the plot now. And even if we did change the plot, it wouldn't be a damned bullshit love story. Now tell me, you're joking with me, right?"

"I'm not joking, Arnie. I've got a great opening. This guy walks into a bar... well, a restaurant—"

"Don't tell me this, Vincent. I don't want to hear about a guy walking into a bar. I want to hear about how the psycho chick goes about killing everyone. Don't do this to me, Vincent. I can't take this."

"I'm sorry, Arnie. I really want to write a love story."

"That's it, I've had enough. I'm coming up to see you. I'll be there later tonight and you'd better have a bunch of pages written about how a lady killer is knocking off a lot of guys. Goodbye."

Arnie disconnected the call.

I sucked down several swallows of whiskey and stared at the walls. I had no idea how to write another psycho killer story. I was fresh out of psycho stories.

The more I thought about his visit, though, the better I felt about it. Maybe it was a good thing that Arnie was coming up to visit me. I'd been cooped up in the house alone for so long, I had forgotten what the outside world was like. Yeah, I reasoned, it would be good to have some company — just so long as he didn't transform into some kind of monster.

Just one minor problem, though. He was expecting several pages of a murder mystery. All I had was ten pages of a love story synopsis. A good one, mind you, but a love story, not a murder mystery. Maybe I could dig deep into my former misanthropic heart and drive out another murder mystery for his sake. I emptied the bottle after that unsettling thought.

I went to the closet and retrieved a fresh bottle of liquid brainpower. I took a long slug. It's always amazed me how the first swig from a fresh bottle always tastes the best.

I sat down at the computer. The screen had timed out and was blank. I pressed the space bar, reactivating it. All was there, as I expected. Well, to be honest, I half expected the glitch to show up again, but it hadn't.

"That's what I'm talking about!" I shouted in joyful realization. I took another swallow.

I looked at my watch. It was 9:12 in the morning. If Arnie left his office in Denver right away, he'd be arriving in only a few hours, so he must be leaving later in the day to arrive here tonight. It was a weekday, after all. He must need to get some work done before heading out to my place.

Liberally speaking, then, I had nine or ten hours to hammer out some kind of murder mystery. To do that, I would have to get very serious and think murderously — slip deep into *sympathetic transference.*

Sympathetic transference, a term I had coined in my first murder mystery, was a self-developed technique I used to put myself in the mood, mind, and being of a murderer — to see through the eyes of a crazed killer, as it were, in order to visualize the actions and state of being necessary for one to commit the heinous crime of willfully taking a life.

In the past it was often a very effective technique involving stern mind control and emotional empathy.

But with the advent of strong drink into my life, I had little mind control and even less empathy. My every waking minute, it seemed, had been consumed by more spiritual pursuits, such as discovering the most efficient means to introduce God Jack into this willful sinner's body.

At that moment I wished Carla, the real Carla, not the werewolf Carla, would return and start smacking me around. Nothing got my murderous juices flowing like a good Carla smackathon. I stopped and thought about that and decided I really needed to seek out some professional help with my psychological being after this synopsis was completed. I was beginning to believe I truly might have some kind of malignant psychosis brewing in my noggin. I swallowed another long stream of whiskey.

My psychosis departed. It was all in my head.

I got serious about my job at hand. "You want a murder story, Arnie? Okay, buddy. You're gonna get a good one. Think murder, Vinnie!" I shouted.

A knock at the door staved off my murderous thoughts.

I looked up at the glass in the front door panel and recognized the intruder of my creative domain. It was Sheriff Overly.

I opened the door and smiled. "Hi ya, Dell."

"Jesus, Mary, and Joseph, Vincent. You look like shit. You look like you went to battle and lost." He sniffed at the air. "You smell like death, too, *again*."

"Sorry, Dell. I have had a battle or two, but I won."

"Not from where I'm standing. I brought you the battery charger like I said I would. If you'll open your garage door for me, I'll hook it up for you."

"Thanks, Dell. Yeah, sure. I'll meet you there. I gotta hit the button."

"Okay."

Dell turned around and headed down the steps to the garage.

I closed the front door and went to the basement stairs that connected to the garage. I descended the stairs and hit the button and heard the garage door open. I reached for my jacket on the hook next to the door when I heard Dell screech, "Good God Almighty!"

I put on my coat and opened the door. "What the hell you screeching like that for, Dell?" I asked, walking out the door.

I got about four steps toward the opened garage door when I noticed a large dark stain on the floor. Looking down, I gasped.

"Jesus Christ!" I shrieked. "What the hell is this?"

I looked up into Dell's eyes. It was like he had seen a ghost.

"Where did this come from, Dell?" I asked, walking around to the front of my backed-in SUV. When I saw the source of the stain, I jumped back in fright and shock.

Lying on the concrete floor of my garage was the nude, decaying body of my ex-girlfriend, Carla, lying in a pool of dried blood.

"Carla!" I bellowed and then moved to her side. "How did this happen?" That's when I noticed the silver candelabra sticking out of her chest.

"Holy shit, Dell!" I shouted.

"Don't touch her, Vincent! This has officially become a crime scene now."

"Crime scene? But Dell, I don't know anything about this!" I insisted.

"Vincent, I'd advise you not to say another word. Not until you get yourself some legal counsel. This is bad."

"Bad? Hell yes, this is bad! How could this happen?"

"I don't know, Vincent, but from the looks of her body, she's been here a while. A few months, looks like."

"Dell, I had nothing to do with this. I mean, last night I thought she showed up, but then she went all werewolf on me and attacked me. I had to stab her in the chest with a silver candelabra, but this morning I realized it was just one of my hallucinations. They're getting worse every day."

"Vincent, you really need to keep silent. Anything you say to me I must report. This don't look good, Vincent. This don't look good at all."

"You don't think I did this, do ya, Dell?"

"I ain't sayin' nothing, Vincent. I ain't sayin' you did or you didn't. I'm just sayin' this don't look good at all for ya. I gotta call this in. You stand right there and don't go near her. You hear me?"

"I won't, Dell. Dear God, this can't be happening."

Sheriff Overly went to his car. He reached inside and pulled out his microphone and began talking to someone on the other end.

He was too far away for me to hear the conversation, but I guessed this day wasn't going to end well for me. I felt the bottle in my hand. I lifted it to my mouth and drank a long tug on it. It didn't help at all. I drank another few swallows. Nothing. Hell, I thought, I need to drown this bad feeling. I drank several more swallows. No effect.

Dell stopped talking. He dropped the microphone back into his front seat and walked toward me.

"I'm sorry, Vincent. I gotta take you into custody. And stop drinking right now. That might just be the problem."

The problem? I thought. How can Brother Jack be the problem? He ain't the problem. He's my solution. I lifted the bottle to my lips again and swallowed all I could until Dell reached up and tried to take the bottle out of my hand.

My mind snapped again.

"Don't you dare touch my bottle!" I screamed. Without thinking, I swung my now nearly empty bottle at Dell's head. It shattered against his skull and split his head open. Blood gushed out and his body hit the concrete floor and didn't move.

"Dell!" I shouted. "God, Dell, I'm so sorry. I didn't mean it, Dell."

I dropped to my knees and tried to stop the gush of blood with my hands. My efforts had no effect. The thick blood flowed through my fingers and ended up as a growing puddle at my feet, spreading out wide and combining with Carla's pool of dried blood. I shook him hard, trying to awaken him. It was no use. Dell Overly was dead as nails right there on the concrete floor of my garage right next to Carla's decaying body.

My brain was working only minimally at that point, but the next thought that came to me was that he had called in to his office. That could only mean that others were on their way to my house and would be there soon.

How the hell was I going to explain two bodies in my garage and one of them the sheriff himself? In the state of mind I had been in over the last few months, maybe I did kill Carla and just didn't remember it. I could just see the headlines in newspapers all over the country: "*Number One Best-selling Author Now Number One Serial Killer Suspect.*"

What the hell was I going to do?

I panicked, but the solution came to me straight out of the darkest depths of the most primitive of places within me. I had to kill everyone who came out here and dispose of them and their vehicles. I had to clean up the mess and get rid of the bodies completely. I couldn't leave a trace of anything for anyone to find. I shifted instantly into survival mode.

I sobered up almost immediately. I hated that. I couldn't have that. So I went to my closet and withdrew another bottle. I sucked down several large swallows. I needed to get re-drunk again very quickly.

My hunting rifle! I suddenly recalled my hunting rifle in the closet of my bedroom. It was a beauty, too, a Winchester Model 70 with a ten-power Leupold telescopic sight. I knew Jack would give me my answers.

I fetched it from the closet and loaded it. I needed to find someplace to hide so I could ambush whoever showed up. I didn't need to worry about anyone hearing the shots; I was miles away from the next living soul on this mountain. Besides, up here it was common to hear gunshots because most of the townsfolk came up here often to fire off some rounds just for the fun of it.

I could do this. I was sure of it. I could pull this off and be back writing my synopsis within a few hours.

* * * * *

The first vehicle to arrive was another patrol car. It came to a stop behind the sheriff's car.

Deputy Ham Cummings exited the vehicle and looked around for Sheriff Overly. Failing to see any sign of him, Deputy Cummings walked toward the steps leading up to my front door. He climbed the steps slowly, looking about him nervously.

"Dell!" he shouted. "Dell! It's me, Ham."

My bullet struck him squarely in the back, severing his spine, and exploded out of his chest, destroying his heart on the way. His body contorted horribly from the impact. I doubt he heard the report of the rifle shot, but even if he did, it was too late. He was dead already, standing there teetering a bit before falling backward and tumbling down the steps to the concrete landing.

The echo of the shot quickly faded into the mountain air until all again was silent and still. I had picked the perfect spot to ambush him. Hidden away up here on the starting line of a thick growth of trees, I had a handy stump to rest my rifle on. The stump made for a perfect rest at the perfect height. I was about a hundred feet from the driveway, perfect for a sniper's nest with a clear, unobstructed view of my yard.

My victims wouldn't know I was here until it was too late. I grabbed the bottle and swallowed three good hits of stabilizing tonic. I hated to kill Ham. He was a good guy. We'd had many good laughs together. But I wasn't going to prison for murder. Not for anything or anyone. I resolved to follow through with what I knew I had to do.

Like it or not, I was now a murderer, twice over; who knows, maybe thrice. And before this day was done, I knew I was going to kill again.

Mind you, these killings were not just words on a page of some fictional story. These bodies were not just characters made up in the mind of an author to give the story a genuine feel. These were real bodies. Three of them at present and more surely to follow soon.

I was in big trouble. I knew it clearly enough.

Three more mouthfuls of whiskey slid down my throat just as the medical examiner's SUV drove into the yard and stopped behind the deputy's car. Doctor Solar Jenkins, the county medical examiner, and Preston McDonald, his assistant, exited the vehicle. Old Solar was well known throughout the area. His nickname was Doc Sunshine.

Both men, too, were surprised at the silence, lack of activity, and a body — the body they were brought out here to examine.

It was Preston McDonald who noticed the deputy's body lying at the foot of the steps. He rushed over to it and with one quick look saw that the deputy had been murdered.

As he turned toward his boss, his chest appeared large and full in my telescopic sight. I squeezed the trigger. The bullet exploded out of his back, taking chunks of his heart with it before he could shout out a warning to his boss. He fell instantly dead.

The report of the rifle startled the medical examiner. He stopped in his tracks and turned around toward the direction of the rifle report.

His faced filled my scope. I squeezed the trigger and watched the bullet strike him directly in the center of his forehead and explode out the back of his head. He was dead before his body hit the ground as well.

The air fell silent once more.

Several minutes and several swallows later, the car from the crime investigation unit came to a stop behind the medical examiner's vehicle. Doctor Michael Roberts exited the vehicle and began his walk toward the house.

He didn't make it four feet past the front bumper of his car. My bullet entered his right temple and disintegrated the entire left side of his head in the same instant. He didn't know he was dead while falling forward toward the ground, but he most definitely was. His body smacked the dry dirt and gravel, sending a cloud of dust into the air.

I walked slowly out from the woods, sucking on my bottle of Jack Daniel's. It well proved itself to be an excellent stress reducer, because I emerged smiling, relaxed, and feeling like a million bucks.

I walked the grounds admiring my skillful work for several minutes, feeling my actions to be sorely regretted but positively justified. Killing Dell was an unfortunate accident, but I saw that as no reason for spending the rest of my life in prison. As for the others, well, they were merely the results of unintended consequences — collateral damage. I wasn't going to prison for them either.

I heard a voice from somewhere say, *"Oh, wicked am I who condones the wickedness you do."*

I twisted my head around, looking for the source. I was alone. At least I believed I was alone.

The words made a lot of sense, but they were spoken too late. I had already convinced myself that in the final analysis my actions were totally warranted. Just in case I was delusional, however, I twisted around trying to find the source of those words once more. I didn't have to look far this time. I was still alone and now certain that they had come from me. I was indeed delusional — again.

I've got to get this drinking under control, I thought. I knew I had to do something to either turn this unfortunate condition around or accept the fact that my psychosis would only worsen. It was becoming a serious problem for me. I'd work on it. I promised myself to get a better handle on it just as soon as I had the time. I would put my mind to work on it and I'd bring it under full control.

I was good at lying to myself.

Now to get rid of all the bodies and evidence.

CHAPTER 6

The medical examiner's SUV bounced and shimmied up the mountain road. Thanks to the battery charger Dell had delivered to me earlier that morning, I would soon have my own SUV running again. Perhaps just in time to make a clean getaway if the need arose. Who was I kidding? Sooner or later I would have to leave everything I owned behind and run for my life. My life wasn't worth a plugged nickel right now, but it was *my* worthless life. That was reason enough.

The ME's rig was perfect for carrying all the bodies up to the cliff at Lake Elizabeth. It moved slowly but effortlessly over the ruts and burrows cut deep in the road by the weather until it came to a stop at the edge of the sharp cliff which dropped off cleanly into the high mountain lake. The same edge I had spent many hours sitting on, writing. It was a real shame that it now had to become a dumping ground for murdered innocents. I was disgusted with myself, but not ready to throw away what little life I still had left.

I pulled the candelabra from Carla's chest and hurled it far out over the cliff and watched it fall into the lake. I did it just in case someone found her body floating in the lake before it sank to the bottom. I didn't want there to be any evidence connecting me to her murder. Not that anyone would have connected the candelabra to me, but why take chances. There was enough connection to me to begin with already.

I put a rock on the gas pedal, revving up the engine. I reached in with my foot and stepped on the brake. I then shifted the gear into drive, removed my foot from the brake, and slammed the door closed as the SUV took off quickly. It ran straight and true toward the cliff's edge, about thirty feet away, and flew off it cleanly.

I trotted over and watched it tumble and roll until it hit the water and sank almost immediately.

I was proud of my masterful accomplishment. "That should do nicely," I remember saying admiringly.

Of course now, having ditched the truck, I had to walk the full five miles back down to my house.

"I can do this," I mumbled to myself.

* * * * *

Arriving at my house about an hour and a half later, I immediately went about cleaning every inch of my garage and yard until there remained not a trace of blood or tissue anywhere. I burned everything I could in the fifty-five-gallon barrel I had used often to burn fall leaves and other refuse. It worked very well with the bloodied rags and other items involved in my cover-up.

Overall, I must say, I did an excellent cleaning job. Even the concrete floor in the garage was as clean as a whistle after a hard scrubbing and the employment of various chemicals good at removing bloodstains and tissue. No one even looking closely at it would see any kind of evidence that a body had been rotting there. A sense of pride and accomplishment filled my being. Not too bad for an alkie, I thought.

Now came the more difficult part of my cover-up. I had to take each remaining vehicle up the mountain and drive it off the cliff into the lake.

This part of my plan was going to be no fun at all, for it meant three more five-mile hikes were in my immediate future. The first wasn't too bad, but I was in no condition to do it several times in the same day. Regardless of that fact, though, that was exactly what I was going to have to do if I had any chance of pulling this off.

After calculating the first round trip, I figured it would take me a good six hours to finish my task, assuming no one else came snooping around.

That's what concerned me most. Arnie was expected near dark. If he by chance arrived before I could complete my task, I might be forced to add another body and car to the lake. This could get even uglier quickly. I liked Arnie. He had been a great agent, as agents go. I couldn't have asked for a better one, but I wasn't about to let him see evidence that might put me behind bars for the rest of my life, or worse. It was simple. It was a cold-hearted truth. If he arrived in the middle of my cover-up efforts, I'd have to eliminate him as well. Jack Daniel's said so, and Jack had never lied to me.

Of course the added risk to all of my efforts was that the sheriff and the others would very soon be missed. Their offices would no doubt try to get them on their radios, but sooner or later, having failed to do so, they'd send out other patrol cars to their last known location. That would be my house, no doubt. I therefore had no time to lose.

* * * * *

Twenty miles, no matter how you slice it, is a very long way to walk in one afternoon. The first ten were difficult, the third five were horrible, and the last five were excruciating. Thank goodness Jack made each trip at least tolerable. But by four o'clock that afternoon, I, Vincent Hobbs, best-selling author and now maniac serial murderer, had successfully pulled off the impossible. Of course, I could barely walk the last few steps down my driveway to my house at the end of my task. But I had made it.

The steps leading up to the deck and my front door presented me with the very last obstacle to completing my short but brilliantly conducted crime spree.

It was beyond painful, but I negotiated each step very carefully and surely, one at a time. After several minutes of agonizing effort, I finally reached the top step. By then, I had to effectively drag each foot individually forward, cursing like a drunken sailor at the pain, inch by inch, toward the front door, but I did it.

I got through the door and slowly worked my way to the closet to retrieve another bottle of courage and inspiration, and then hobbled to my sofa, where I collapsed, with a groan and two aching sighs, into the comfort of those soft cushions.

As I drank my fill of whiskey, my mind would not rest from asking the same question over and over. Who killed Carla and then dumped her body on my garage floor?

I knew plain enough, by then, that it could not have been me. Drunk or not, I knew I hadn't seen Carla in months, with the exception of my recent werewolf battle. She had never attempted to contact me by phone and she certainly had never shown herself at my door. But that *was* my candelabra sticking out of her chest. I knew that much to be true. Still, my eyes glanced up at the mantel just to be sure. Yep, the candelabra was missing now. The last time I checked, after the werewolf attack, it was there. How could I have missed that? And if Sheriff Overly was right and her body had been there for several months, I should have missed the candelabra long before the werewolf battle. No, I reassured myself, I did not kill Carla.

Beyond that, I was strangely in love with her. The thought of killing Carla had never entered my mind, even after she smacked me around the way she had. In fact, getting smacked was exotically erotic, thrilling even. The thought of getting angry and retaliating never entered my mind.

But she was dead and someone had gone to a lot of trouble, using my candelabra to kill her to make me out to be the guilty party.

As an author of murder mysteries, it was actually quite a brilliant plan. I'd have to file this whole experience away for use in a future book. If I ever wrote another book. That is, if I got away with all of this in the first place.

Still, someone had gone well out of their way to find her, kill her, and transport her body to my home simply to implicate me in her murder for some nefarious reason lost to me at the moment. But why would anyone do that to her? For what purpose? To what end? It seemed a lot of effort for an extortion plot. But then, I had heard of stranger plots throughout my life.

Funny, though, for I had never received any threats or attempts at extortion. In fact, the only calls I had received over the last two or three months had been from Arnie, pestering me about the synopsis.

"Holy crap!" I shouted. "Arnie could be here any minute and I don't have anything written." He would be so pissed.

I didn't know what to do. Panic began to form in my mind just as I noticed the blinking light on my answering machine. I pushed the button to listen to it. It was Arnie.

"Hey, kid, I know I said I'd be up there today, but I'm tied up in negotiations. I can't make it up there. I'll try to come up tomorrow if I can clear my calendar. I'll call you tomorrow sometime and touch base with you. Meanwhile, get writing a good murder piece. Talk to you later, Vincent."

Oh happy day, I thought. Arnie had postponed his trip. That meant that I could recover from my death march and still have tomorrow to scribble up something that might satisfy him.

* * * * *

The sun had dropped into the trees. Within an hour it would be pitch black. I felt suddenly safe and assured that all was going to be okay now. For a moment, though, I once again felt really bad about killing Dell and the others. I really liked Dell and Ham. I never knew the others, but I'm sure someone somewhere this evening was worried sick about them.

Still, Dell had broken the sacred rule for alcoholics. You never try to take the bottle from the hand of an alkie. That could get you killed. I smirked. It *did* get someone killed. How strange is that? No matter now. It was clearly the wrong move on his part. I wouldn't let anyone do that and get away with it.

But then again, it certainly was not reason enough to kill the man. Hey, I reminded myself, it was done now. There was nothing I could do about it. I just had to move on, find a way to get past it.

I was thinking about how painful it would be to try and get up and go out to the hot tub and soak the pain out of my legs, but it sounded like a great idea. And just what Doctor Jack prescribed. Just as I began to make the attempt to rise up off the sofa, I saw a pair of lights flash across the walls of my great room.

I knew instantly who it was. It was another sheriff's deputy come to ask about Dell and the others. I gave it serious thought for a moment and tried to calm myself. No, killing him was not the answer. Besides, I'd never make the walk back from the lake. I couldn't even make it to the door to answer it.

I told myself to act as if all was normal and everything might just turn out fine. If he wanted to look around, be friendly, inviting, accommodating. I had taken great care to eliminate any incriminating evidence. Let the fool look around if he wanted.

A knock on my door brought my mind back from wandering. I tried to get up but my legs protested too much.

"Come on in," I shouted. "It's unlocked."

The door opened and in stepped Deputy John Burns. "County Sheriff, Mister Hobbs!" he shouted.

I knew him. "Over here, John. On the sofa. Forgive me, please. I'd get up, but my legs are in full rebellion. Started a new exercise program today walking a few miles. Now I wish I'd never started."

The deputy chuckled.

"I know how you feel, Mister Hobbs. I hate the first few days." He walked around to the front of the sofa. He must have noticed the pain on my face because he scrunched his nose and shook his head. "You like you're about to die from pain."

"I am. I can't move. I think dying would be the kind thing."

I raised my bottle up to my lips and swallowed a good bit. "But thanks to Jack here, I might get through the night without crying too much."

He laughed. Then he got serious.

"I'm looking for Dell. Have you seen him?"

I knew better than to full-out lie about it. A little truth is better than complete bullshit. "Yeah," I said. "Dell dropped by this morning and dropped off his battery charger for me. I haven't driven in such a long time, the damn battery died."

"That's it?"

I pretended to think a second or two. I made it look good. "Well, he sat and had a cup of coffee with me too. But he said he couldn't stay too long. He had a busy day today."

"That's strange, Mister Hobbs. We recorded a call earlier today telling us about a body up here."

"Here? Are you kidding me?"

"No, sir. The radio call said he found a body in your garage and he wanted the medical examiner and a crime unit sent up here pronto."

"That doesn't sound like a good joke to me, John. I don't think it's very funny."

"We don't think so either. He hasn't answered any of our calls all day. Would you mind if I had a look around?"

"Hell no, John. Look anywhere you want to. If you don't mind, though, could I not follow you around? My legs are killing me. I'd hate for you to see a grown man cry like a baby."

"Sure, Mister Hobbs. You could remain right here. Where is the garage door opener?"

"Ah, yeah. Go down the hallway there, John, and then down the stairs. The garage door opener is on the wall next to the door."

"Okay. Thanks. I'll be right back."

"Take your time, John. I ain't going anywhere."

I took a big chug of Jack. It calmed me nicely.

I had a new thought.

"Hey, John! Before you go, could you help me get to my computer table? I don't think I can make it on my own."

"Sure thing," he said.

With his help and despite my many shrieks of pain, I managed to get into the chair in front of my computer. I thanked him and he left me to go to the garage.

As I sat there waiting for the computer to boot up, those nagging questions again filled my inebriated mind. Who killed Carla and dumped her body in my garage? And why?

The computer booted up and I clicked on my document. When it opened, I almost screamed.

What I had written the day before was gone, in its place another story. As I read it, my stomach quaked. If I could have run, I would have run to the toilet and vomited.

The story was an exact recitation of the events of the day. The murders and the disposing of the evidence. It was exact. Not a piece of the story was missing, glorified, or embellished. I drank more whiskey, more to keep myself from heaving my guts out all over the place than for any other reason.

I fought through the pain in my legs and stood up. Nearly crying from misery, I went to the kitchen sink and reached for the faucet handle. I flushed my face with cold water, trying to regain the blood flow to my brain.

When I looked up, the deputy was just approaching the computer table from the front door. I hadn't even heard it open.

I tried to move, but my legs were like knives. I groaned and yelped.

"You need some help, Mister Hobbs?"

In truth, I felt almost paralyzed from pain.

"Give me a second, John. I feel like my legs are going to fall off my body."

"Give me a shout when you're ready."

Then John began reading the story on the screen. I had forgotten to close the lid before I came to the kitchen. Jesus Christ, I thought, if he gets to reading too much, I'm a dead man. No, *he's* a dead man.

I fought through the pain and started to move toward the computer. I nearly collapsed. John noticed and rushed to help me. He got me to the chair at the computer table. I closed the lid nonchalantly, almost in a teasing way. "Hey," I said, "You can't read that. It's bad luck to read a story before it's finished."

The deputy chuckled. "From what I did read, it looks like it's going to be another winner for you."

"Thanks, John. You know how a writer's mind works, making up crazy shit all the time. It's a disease, you know."

John chuckled again. "I have a tough time writing reports. I can't imagine how you big-time authors do it over and over again. It's amazing."

"Well, thanks, John. I appreciate the kind words. Did you see what you needed to see? In the garage, I mean."

"Yeah. Sorry. I sort of forgot about it. Yes, sir. You're right. That's Dell's battery charger down there. I recognize it."

"Do you want to take it back now?"

"No, it's okay. I could see that it's not quite finished."

"I could bring it in to the station tomorrow if you want."

"That's between Dell and you. I'll let Dell decide. I just wish I knew what happened to him."

"Just a guess here, John, but maybe the radio call got screwed up somehow. Maybe it sounded like he was talking about my place, but it was someplace else. Maybe the call was somewhere where he doesn't get a good radio signal. You know these mountains out here can be buggers with radios."

"I listened to it myself. I'm sure he was talking about your place."

"Well, John, did you see any bodies down there?"

"Nope. Sure didn't."

"Then *you'll* have to explain the radio call, because I sure can't."

"The thing, though. The medical examiner and his assistant, the crime unit guy, Doc Roberts, and Deputy Cummings are all missing as well."

"Damn!" I said, sounding like a polished actor. "If that isn't strange. I sure hope Dell and the others are okay."

"Me too. Well, sorry to trouble you. You think you'll be okay? I mean you look like you want to cry every time you move."

"I feel like crying, but I'll be fine, John. I'll work a bit more and then I'll battle my way to the hot tub and soak all the hurt out of me. Thanks for your help, though. In a few days I'll be walking just fine. Hell, in a month or two I'll be running these roads around here."

"I bet you do. Okay, Mister Hobbs, I'll get out of your hair. Thanks for letting me look around. You have a good night, sir."

"Anytime, John. You're always welcome out here. Say hello to Dell for me when you find him."

"Will do, sir. Good night. I'll let myself out."

John left, closing the door behind him.

Okay, I have to say it. I know it sounds arrogant as hell, but I'm freakin' good. "Say hello to Dell for me." That was bold-ass brilliant, and I don't mind saying so.

I murdered five people today, disposed of six bodies, and the vehicles, and I'm still sitting in my own house like an innocent man. And damn, with winter just around the corner, the snow will fall and the lake will freeze. With any luck at all, those bodies will never be found. Hell, they're inside the SUV. They won't be going anywhere. I hated to do it, but I had no choice.

A sick feeling swept over me again. I remembered the story. I opened the screen and tapped the space bar. The story came up again. I scrolled through a few more pages until I came upon another warning.

"I KNOW WHAT YOU DID. I KNOW WHERE THE BODIES ARE. FINISH THE STORY OR LAW ENFORCEMENT WILL BE ALERTED."

"Dear God," I mumbled to myself. "I'm screwed."

A second or two later another message popped up on the screen:

"YES. I AM NOW THE MASTER."

CHAPTER 7

"*You're never greeted by more than what you've created.*"

Those prophetic words, spoken by one of my earlier characters in a bullshit philosophical book that sold a total of five copies worldwide, came flying back to smack me right in the kisser.

It felt like a physical slap. I looked around for Carla. She wasn't there. It was the slap of my own reality. I took a drink to eradicate that veracity. My hallucinations were seemingly real enough. I could do without the slapping ones.

I had written the book, oh, about two lifetimes ago, it seemed. Now those stinking words returned to haunt me.

Was it true, though? Had I really created everything that had been happening to me over the last couple of days? To be honest, I wasn't sure, but I had little doubt that my drinking was getting well out of hand by then. I had even less doubt that my decision-making ability had been very much impaired of late through the infusing of whiskey with my blood, most likely blocking the oxygen from getting to my brain.

It all made sense. No, it didn't. Nothing made any sense whatsoever. The computer screen had announced that someone thought they had become my master. Oh, really?

The master? Who's the master? Who's doing this? I asked myself. What the hell is happening?

Sure, I was mostly in the bag while trying to reason out an answer. And my brain was no doubt pickled by an inordinate amount of alcohol. But as I had already known before, I was somehow a functioning alcoholic. On a minimal basis, to be sure, but I was functioning. I knew what I was doing. The choice to drink was mine. I could stop at any time. I could put the bottle down and walk away whenever I decided to do so.

Of course, I had no such idiotic thoughts of doing that. That would be like throwing the baby out with the dirty bathwater. I mean, even if I had stopped drinking that very moment, I'd still have to deal with having murdered five people and then disposing of their bodies. No, my buddy Jack Daniel's was right where he should be, where he needed to be, right where *I* needed him to be, his neck in my hand, ready to soothe my worried mind.

Speaking of slaves and masters, answer me this. Just what is an alcoholic anyway? If that definition includes the ability to walk away from it all, then I was indeed an alcoholic. But if it did not include that ability, then I proclaim for all the world to hear that I am not an alkie.

Between you and me, though, I was as alcoholic as they come. But I liked deceiving myself. I liked the feeling a temporary, albeit self-induced, reprieve gave me. It freed the spirit, although there was little hope for the mind, it being forever mired in self-subterfuge.

Applying the previous proclamation to novel writing, then, I am an author, the creator of stories. As such, I determine my plotlines and I dictate how my characters react to such plots. In this, then, I am the master, my characters slaves to my whim and fancy.

You see, even using an alcohol-sodden brain, I understood the ramifications of such thinking. I also understood that without a slave there could be no master. I had heard it said before: "If you're not in charge of your own life, who is?" In my case, however, it was anybody's guess.

Those words, too, came back to me like a whack on the cheek, the face cheek. (I just wanted to be clear about that once again to avoid getting into an indelicate discussion about spankings. Now I'm blushing.)

As far as I knew at that moment, I was in charge of my own life. To wit, I was master of how and why I reacted the way I did to the circumstances that had befallen me lately.

And if I was living under my own control, then I was not a slave. And if I was not a slave, then whoever was manipulating my computer was certainly no master.

If, after all the craziness, I still possessed the ability to walk away cleanly, then, indeed, I was most certainly the master, albeit master over a slave of one... namely, me. But that might confuse you, so ignore that last part. Although that might be difficult now that I have already raised the notion.

Anyway, if I was master, then it followed that whoever was claiming to be master couldn't be meaning mastery over me.

But whoever it was attempting to manipulate me did seem to know about the murders and such. In their own sick mind perhaps they considered the secret to give them the power to control me and my actions.

So, to arrogantly say that I was still the full master over my own destiny might not have been the whole truth of the matter.

Consider this, though. Why did the so-called master feel the need to live in the shadows? A true master would not hesitate to step out into the light and proudly profess his power and might — to establish his position as master.

Not this supposed master, apparently. He hid behind a computer. And that told me something about who it might be. By that I mean to continue hiding from me, he demonstrated uncertainty as to whether or not he was yet the master. He still had doubts, it seemed.

I became a bit brazen and spoke my question. "Who are you that believes he is master?"

Seconds later I received a strange response on the computer screen:

"ASK INSTEAD WHO WAS MASTER OF RENÉ LE CHANT."

Then the computer screen began flashing **"RENÉ LE CHANT"** over and over until it filled the screen and then started scrolling, repeating the name.

After a time I struck the 'escape' key and the scrolling abruptly stopped.

Then my mind kicked in. I knew that name. I knew it well.

René Le Chant was an obscure author who died in Paris in 1610. He died rather young and was largely forgotten shortly after his death; in fact, he wasn't at all popular in his own day.

Only a handful of the most ardent, dyed-in-the-wool mystery writers have even heard of him. I'm one. I might be his biggest fan. He was a mystery writer. He wrote crime novels styled much like today's, far ahead of their time, but they were not well received. To be honest, they were not very well written. In fact, it was a true wonder how any of them ever got published at all.

He died mysteriously. At first it was believed that he was a victim of murder. But when the Paris police, or whatever the hell their outfit was called back then, investigated his death, they discovered a piece of paper under his body on the floor. On it were the penned words "The story." They were the only words on the piece of paper and they appeared to be written in Le Chant's own handwriting. No one could understand what significance, if any, those words had, nor what part, if any, they had in his death.

After a brief investigation the authorities concluded that Le Chant's death was a suicide, not a murder. They speculated that his failure as an author led him into a deep melancholy. In that state of despair, he chose to end his life rather than live with his disappointment. Although they offered neither proof nor substantial reasoning for such a conclusion, that's how it went into the official record: "Death by misadventure or suicide."

Sometime later it was found that the corner pages of his favorite book had been poisoned. One of the policemen had absconded with the book and died while reading it. It was then suggested that Le Chant, too, had ingested the poison when he licked his fingers to turn the pages, just like the policeman. Arsenic, said some. Cyanide, said others. Still others insisted it was strychnine that did in both men, considering the odd contortion of both bodies. Whatever the poison used, it was effective.

Many of Le Chant's "miserable" stories, as he labeled them in a letter to a friend shortly before his death, apparently died with him. There are no novels in print today, and only three books are known to even be in existence, and I own one of them. The original title is *L'horrible Fin d'un Psychotique.* I am told that it best translates into English as *The Awful End of a Psychotic.* It fits, doesn't it? It's me. I mean, you can see what influenced me to become a murder mystery writer. I bought it for $2,500 while on vacation in

Paris a couple of years ago. I considered it a good deal then, and I still do.

To close out my thoughts on this issue, it had been said that all of his original manuscripts have disappeared as well. The only things written by him that remain are some letters.

I tried to reason why someone would bring up the name of an obscure, long-dead author. It made no sense to me. He was certainly no master of literature, not from the copies I've read. But that's not what the words said on the screen. They stated, "Ask instead who was master of René Le Chant."

Those words caused me to swallow whiskey by the mouthfuls. "Who was master of René Le Chant?"

I had no knowledge that ever indicated Monsieur Le Chant had had a master, or a tutor, or even some kind of sponsor, or mentor, for that matter. At least no one I would consider to have exercised a 'master-like' authority over him at that time. But then, as I noted earlier, he was largely an obscure man who had had no impact on the book world whatsoever. So information regarding his life was meager and woefully incomplete. Perhaps there was much more to the story of his life and death than anyone could have ever guessed.

I thought about it a bit more, and finally I had had enough. "Ghost stories," I said aloud. "Are you suggesting that all of this has been caused by the ghost of this René Le Chant?"

Seconds later, more words appeared on the screen.

"SEEK HIS MASTER AND YOU SHALL KNOW WHO IS MASTER NOW."

I abruptly realized that a new twist in our communications had occurred without me grasping it. I had spoken words before without catching on to the change. Indeed, I no longer needed to type my responses. I could speak aloud my thoughts. Someone had my house wired for sound. That *really* pissed me off. It also scared the hell out of me. I tried to be brave, however.

"Why don't you kiss my ass," I blurted out.

"FINISH THE STORY, OR ELSE!"

"Or else what, dipshit?" I shouted.

The response was still confined to my laptop screen, I noted. There was no response to my immediate challenge.

"What are you going to do if I don't?" I continued verbally. "Oh, that's right, you'll call the law on me. Go ahead. Call the law. But you won't, will ya? If I'm in prison, who's gonna finish the story? You need me, don't you?"

"FINISH THE STORY, OR ELSE!"

"Bite me!"

"FINISH THE STORY!"

"No! Now who's the master, bitch?"

The computer screen stayed blank.

I waited for several more minutes. No further response.

"That's what I'm talking about!" I yelled. "I'm writing a love story. Arnie's gonna love it. I'll sell millions of books. *I am master of my own life! Live with it!*"

I felt uplifted. Then another thought filled my head and I asked it aloud.

"Did you kill Carla?"

I waited for a response. There was none.

"Did you kill Carla? I demand to know."

No response.

"That's what I thought. You *did* kill her. Why? Why did she have to die?"

No response.

I realized that whatever channel of mutual communication had been established earlier was now closed. Still, just to be certain, I pressed further.

"Fine. Have it your way, but one thing is clear to me now. You're no master, except over your own delusional state of mind. You're pathetic, you know that?"

I was taunting my adversary. I knew it. I meant to do it, if for no other reason than to see how he or she would respond. I was bold that way. Stupid, but bold. Still, what really bothered me was how they had gained control over my computer in the first place, knowing that I was not connected to the internet. I had been hacked, certainly, but just how that was accomplished escaped me.

It was my writing computer. There was nothing on it of any importance. I kept no personal passwords, codes, or bank account information on it. I used it strictly for writing. True, all of my stories were stored on it, but I had backups of everything. I had double backups. If I were to lose this particular laptop, I'd lose nothing except what I had written that day and had failed to back up.

At the end of each workday, though, like clockwork, drunk or not, I backed up my writing onto a flash drive. That flash drive never stayed connected to the computer. I withdrew it immediately upon backing up an updated file.

Still, and despite all my confidence, it was a bit unnerving to have something so personal as your laptop under the control of someone else.

A nagging question returned. *Just who the hell was this someone else?* I hated that question, but under the circumstances I knew it would return time and time again until I discovered the unwanted spy's identity. Another question then did the breaststroke through my whiskey-filled brain. *Is it at all possible to discover the identity of my secret hacker by any other means than begging for it?*

A bubble of an idea then burst.

CHAPTER 8

Before the mist of the idea evaporated, I scooped up my wireless phone and dialed a number. I impatiently waited for an answer.

"Come on. Come on," I begged.

"Geekmeisters," said a voice on the other end finally. "How can I help you?"

"Thank goodness! Hi, Jerry. This is Vincent Hobbs. How you doing?"

"Hey, Vincent. Not bad. What's going on?"

"I have no idea, but I'm beginning to think my computer has been hacked somehow and someone is having some sick fun with me. But I don't see how. I haven't been online for at least a month. I haven't even checked email."

"Which computer, Vincent? Your desktop or your laptop?"

"My laptop."

"Good. There's nothing on that but your stories, right?"

"You got it."

"Is it on?"

"Yeah. But it's not connected to the internet."

"No problem. Hang on a second. I'll be right back with you."

"Thanks."

I painfully rose up off the chair and began strolling, or more accurately, hobbling (my legs were still in full revolt) around the room aimlessly. I hoped walking around would help heal my aching legs.

While I waited for him to come back on the line, I enjoyed several tugs on the bottle.

His name was Jerry Van Winkle. He owned Geekmeisters. It was a computer build–and-repair store in Fairplay. His primary business was building custom computers and repairing them for the residents, companies, and government offices of Park County. Everyone knew him, but no one truly knew him. I got to know him well enough to know certain undisclosed facts about him.

To look at him, you'd think he was about fifteen years old. But he was twenty-six and a graduate of Harvard with a master's degree in computer science. Just what he was doing hidden away up in Fairplay is a story for another day, but I can say this much about that. He did have a bit of a specialty which, if further discussed, would probably answer any questions as to why he ended up in Fairplay. Anyway, he built both my desktop and laptop computers. He knew them inside and out, literally.

Because it was so far out of town for him to come out and perform maintenance on my computers, which was often, because I was *not* a computer geek every bit as much as he *was* a computer geek, he had installed a very special program and device on my computers that allowed him to get into them remotely and fix things for me even if I wasn't connected to the internet.

Before you think it, the answer is no. No one but Jerry had access to the device. He invented it. He controlled it. He told me so when he installed it. I was certain the hacker was not invading me through that device or program — unless it was Jerry himself. And it wasn't.

Don't ask me how he managed that; it beats the grunt out of me. Besides, if I knew, he'd have to kill me. That's what he said, anyway. He may have been joking about that, but I never wanted to find out the truth of it.

As a matter of general security, the program also was something of a mousetrap. If a hacker attempted to attack my computer, Jerry's program did something special. It not only stopped the attack but also traced down the attacker and disabled their computer. Actually, I'm putting it nicely. Jerry's program wiped out the hacker's computer. I mean it completely fried the hacker's hard drives and motherboard. It could effectively turn an expensive piece of sophisticated computer hardware into a very big doorstop.

Needless to say, his services were in high demand by almost everybody, including Uncle Sam. And since I don't know when to shut the hell up, you've probably now figured out why he made Fairplay his home under the assumed name of Jerry

Van Winkle. Yeah, you guessed it. That wasn't his real name.

"Hey, Vincent, I want you to reboot your computer. I'm going to turn on the monitor program and keep a watch out for anything suspicious. You won't notice anything different. Just go about your normal activity. My program works in the background, as you know. If I get some hits, I'll contact you. Meanwhile, if you see anything strange on your screen, just reboot it. I'll be watching for any odd reconnections."

"Okay, Jerry. Could I connect to the internet and check my email?"

"Sure. Just go about your normal business. I'll get back to you if something strange occurs."

"Thanks, Jerry. I appreciate it."

"No sweat, Vincent. Chat with you later."

I completed my call and walked back to my computer.

On the screen were these words:

"NO SAVING FROM THE KID. FINISH THE STORY OR DIE!"

I sat down and smiled confidently. I knew that this deranged yahoo messing with my computer and me was about to end up with a fried computer.

"You don't scare me, 'cause I got you now, sucker. Keep it up."

I chugged another swallow and grinned.

* * * * *

My writing continued pleasantly and without issue for several hours that day. I made great progress on my new love story, which I had named *The Whisper of Happy Hearts*. I finally sat back in my chair, guzzled a bit of Jack, and sighed. I was pleased.

It had been a hell of a couple days. I'd committed five murders, got away with it cleanly, and got a huge jump on my new book. Of course, I wasn't proud of those murders, but they needed to be done. It was a simple matter of survival. That's how I categorized them. That's how I justified it all; I wasn't about to carry the guilt of them around like a yoke. Things happen from time to time in life. For all concerned, it would be best for me to put it behind me and move into a much better future.

The phone rang. It was Arnie.

"Hey, kid. I think I can make it up there to see you this afternoon. How goes the new book?"

"Great, Arnie! I'm calling it *The Whisper of Happy Hearts*. You like the title?"

"I don't. It doesn't pop for me. How about this? *The Scream of Bloody Hearts*. Now that sounds like a good murder story to me."

"You don't understand, Arnie. It's not a murder mystery I'm writing, it's a love story. I told you that."

"Oh, Christ, Vincent. I told *you* I don't need a love story. I need a murder mystery for the publishers. They're champing at the bit for your next murder story. What are you trying to do, give me an ulcer?"

"Arnie, I'm finished with murder. This is a really great love story. I can't wait until you see it. It will have you sobbing."

"The only sobbing I'll be doing is when they reject your story idea and take with them the advance. Now cut this bullshit out and give me a good murder mystery. You got that? Enough of this love crap. Give me blood and torn bodies. That's what your readers want. That's what they're expecting. That's what the publishers want. And Vincent, it's what *I* want. You understand?"

"I hear you, Arnie. I just don't want to write that crap anymore."

"You want a two-million-dollar advance?"

"Two million? Are you joking?"

"That's where they're at now based on your sales. I can get them higher with a killer synopsis. Would you like that?"

"Sure I would." I did a quick calculation in my head. "That's a million seven."

"Now you're getting it."

"Now I got it."

"Good. Now write me a murder mystery. I'm coming up there tonight. I'd better see the synopsis of an awesome murder mystery, or you and I are going to have a problem. Get it?"

"Got it."

"Okay. I'll be there about five. Get your ass in gear and write."

"Fine. I'll have something for you by then."

"Good."

Arnie hung up abruptly.

I sat back, frustrated. I had in my mind a beautiful love story. But every way I turned, it was like the universe wanted a murder mystery.

I sure could use the money from the advance, I thought. I mean, who couldn't use a million seven? Jack isn't cheap, you know. But to get the advance, I had to earn it. To earn it, I had to write a great synopsis that Arnie could sell. But like I said, I had no idea where to begin a murder mystery. My murder mystery openings had all been used before. I had nothing fresh and witty for him.

I racked my brain for a dynamite opening. Nothing. Then again, I had an opening. A guy walks into a bar. It's a great opening. It's always a great opening to any genre. Okay, I thought. This guy walks into a bar, meets this chick, and she offs him. I had this written already. But then where the hell would the story go after the opening? This is where I had to stop, slug some Jack, and wonder.

Out of the blue it hit me. I mean, it was like a bullet had struck me right between the eyes. I *had* a story. And if properly massaged, it could turn out to be a great story. And wouldn't you know it, the hacker had given it to me. I could steal it. What was he going to do, argue about the copyright? Besides, it was all about me. It was my story. It was a story about how a guy started writing a story and shit began happening to him. DAMN!

I backed up what I had written earlier again, taking no chances. Someday I'd finish the love story, but right now I had to type like mad and retell my story. Of course, I had to change names and circumstances, but, in essence, I'd just retype what the hacker had typed before. I was proud of myself. I'd have something for Arnie to read in plenty of time.

I started typing.

A guy walked into a bar. He spotted the hot number in the darkened corner. Right away he saw that she was a killer. Her looks were killing him already. It didn't matter to him. He was there for a good time, even if it meant his life. And little did he know it would.

CHAPTER 9

I had been lost in thought, so the knock on the door startled me. I turned to look over my shoulder through the glass front door. It was Arnie. He didn't look pleased.

I hobbled to the door and greeted him, carrying my bottle of pain reliever, of course. "Hey, Arnie! Welcome," I groaned.

"You look like shit, kid."

"It's a long story."

"What's the matter with your legs?"

"New exercise program. Just getting started."

"You look like you're about to die."

"You don't know the half of it. Come in, come in."

"Before I do, Vince, I gotta ask. Have you got a murder mystery waiting for me?"

"Boy, do I! Come on in and have a look for yourself."

Arnie walked in. I directed him to the couch.

"Smells like death in here, or piss. I'm not sure which."

"Like I said, you don't know the half of it. By the way, you didn't happen to see a werewolf standing out there, did you?"

"What the hell are you talking about?"

"Forget it. Want a drink?"

"No, thanks. I want to see a synopsis."

"Fine. Take a seat."

He sat down on the couch as I moaned and groaned my way over to my desk to retrieve a stack of paper. I gingerly walked over and handed it to him.

"You should take it easy on that exercise stuff. It doesn't look like it agrees with you."

"The hell you say. In a couple of weeks I'll be sprinting."

"If you live that long."

Boy, did he hit the nail on the head with that remark. But he didn't know it and I wasn't going to start down that road with him unless I was forced to.

"I plan on doing just that," I said, believing it. Well, to some degree at least.

"Let's see what you've got here," he said, flipping through the pages of my synopsis.

"I just finished printing them out. Tell me what you think."

"I will, but move away from me. You really stink. When did you last take a shower?"

"It's been a while, I guess. I can go shower now and let you read in peace."

"Great idea."

I started to shuffle away, still moaning from the pain. He started reading.

"Hey!" he shouted.

I stopped and turned toward him.

"A guy walks into a bar?"

"Keep reading, Arnie. You'll love it."

I left him seated on the couch, reading, while I went into my bathroom to shower and shave.

* * * * *

I walked out into the great room. The shower did me good, and I felt refreshed. My legs still killed me, but the rest of me felt damn good. Of course, I was still in great need of my Doctor Daniel's Pain Reliever.

Arnie was still reading, but he had a glass of Jack neat in his hand. He sipped at it from time to time while his eyes remained glued to the pages. He didn't even notice me returning. He looked like he was enjoying what I had written.

I eased down into the chair at my computer table and remained quiet. That's a lie. I groaned and moaned getting down into the chair and whimpered like a baby, hoping I'd never have to walk down from the lake ever again.

"Holy shit," he mumbled, but kept reading. Then he chuckled lightly and kept reading.

I kept quiet.

Several minutes went by. He sipped at his drink.

"Jesus Christ!" he mumbled again.

He loved it. I could tell.

He remained quiet for the longest time, dropping page after page onto the couch and devouring the words off the next page like a starving man. A million seven was what went through *my* mind.

Finally the last page was in front of his nose. Then it was done. He sat mesmerized for several seconds, staring at the floor.

"Gotcha!" I said.

He looked up at me, almost not seeing me. Then the recognition set in.

"Jesus, Vince!"

"Is that a good Jesus?"

"It's a really good Jesus. It ain't a psycho-killer woman, but wow. You got another number one best seller here for sure. How the hell did you come up with this one?"

"I'm an author, Arnie. It's my job."

"I'll tell you this. Your mind is on another level from the rest of us poor slobs."

"So you think you can sell this one?"

"Sell it? I'll have them tossing in the kitchen sink with everything else I'm gonna take from them. Good job, Vince! Really nice work. That's why you're my number one author, kid. Just amazing!"

His eyes dropped to the floor. Seconds later they were back on me. "So this guy walks into a bar, huh?"

I laughed. "Yep."

"I particularly love the line 'Our eyes met. I sat down. I knew right away just how I was going to kill her.' Damn! That one sent chills up my spine. You're the master, kid."

Just then it struck me. Damn straight I am. I'm the author. I'm the master. I am the goddamned MASTER!

"Glad you liked it, Arnie. How about another drink?"

I could share, I thought. Why not? I had the bottle in my hand. I took a swig just in case he said yes.

"No, thanks, kid. I gotta get back to town. Tomorrow I'm gonna rock a few worlds with this. Give me a couple weeks, and I'll have at least two million or we'll find another publisher."

"Wow! That would be awesome." Hell yeah, I hollered with my inside voice. I did it!

Arnie jumped up from the couch and headed for the door. "Vince, you never cease to amaze me, kid. Good job."

"Thanks, Arnie."

"Hey Vince, how long do you think it'll take to get the first draft written from when I give you the go?"

"Give me thirty days from contract, Arnie."

"Great. I'll tell them that. With the rewriting and editing, that should put it right about Christmastime for the world release if they fast-track it. They'll love the hell outa that. They can start advertising immediately."

I felt ... *accomplished*, if that was the right word. It was all turning for me.

I hobbled Arnie to the steps and stopped. He continued down them with a little skip in his step.

"I'm glad it was worth the drive up here for you, Arnie."

"I'd drive up here tomorrow if it meant you'd have another dilly for me like this," he replied without turning around.

Just then I heard a familiar sound that I hadn't heard in decades. The clippety-clop of a trotting horse. From around the brushy tree came the horse and rider.

As he drew closer, I could swear I recognized him. It was right there at the tip of my brain. The chaps, the black-dyed beaver-skin cowboy hat, the black duster, the black stallion. It all looked strangely familiar.

As the rider came closer, even Arnie stopped in his tracks to stare up at the rider with his dark, steely, piercing eyes and black stubble of a beard. The rider stopped his horse short of Arnie's car and dismounted.

Arnie looked back at me. I just shrugged my shoulders. Hellfire. I had no idea what was going on. I took a long swig. It settled me.

The rider dropped the reins to the ground. The horse stood still. Then he lifted his head and stared at Arnie.

"You fixin' to leave with them papers, friend?"

Arnie blinked. "Papers?" he asked.

"That's what I asked, pardner."

Arnie looked back up at me. I shook my head. His eyes turned back to the dark stranger. "I don't know what you mean, mister."

"Them papers in yer hand, you lying varmint. You fixin' on takin' them with ya, are ya?"

Arnie glanced down at my synopsis in his hand. "Well, yeah. I gotta get them to New York. Who are you, anyway?"

"Jesus Christ!" I yelled. "It can't be. It just can't be."

Arnie looked up at me again, as if asking a silent question. But I just shook my head in silence.

The stranger looked familiar. I hate it when my hallucinations look familiar. Means I've been drinking way too much. But what the hell, there he was, standing there looking bad as can be. Finally I placed him.

"Bart Gamble!" I yelled. "Are you Bart Gamble? Are you the gunfighter called Bart Gamble?"

Arnie's eyes returned to the stranger.

"Who's askin'?" the stranger demanded.

"*I'm* askin'!" I shouted down at him gruffly. "And if you're as smart as I think you are, you'll answer me, or I'll be knowing the reason why."

"What the hell is going on?" yelled Arnie.

"Don't you remember, Arnie? *A Good Day for a Gunfight*? You don't remember?"

Arnie grimaced. "Do you know this asshole?"

I abruptly recognized that he couldn't have been a hallucination. Arnie could see him also. I felt strangely relieved.

"Who you callin' asshole, fancy pants?" asked the stranger.

"Fancy pa—… I'm Arnold Feinstein. Vincent's agent. And yeah, you're an asshole. Get that horse outa my way, or I'll run you both ov—"

Arnie turned his gaze up at me with the queerest look. He grimaced again. "Bart Gamble? Are you kidding me?"

"This ain't no joking matter, ya rascal."

Faster than lightening, the stranger drew his six-gun and shot Arnie once, square in the chest. Arnie dropped to the ground, instantly dead. Then the stranger's eyes turned up toward me.

"Yeah," I said, "that's who you are. Bart Gamble. Gunfighter, robber, gambler, womanizer, and all-around bad egg. The scourge of Park County."

"That's right, Hobbs. I am that and a lot more. All of it bad. As bad as it comes. I'm here for you, too."

Suddenly feeling no pain in my legs at all, I took a long swig and dashed into my house to retrieve my Smith and Wesson 9 mm pistol. It was loaded. It was always loaded. I pulled the slide back and chambered the first round.

I returned to the deck just in time to see that Bart had reached the steps. He looked up at me, scowled, and started climbing. His spurs jingled with each step he took.

His eyes looked cold and dead. His serious expression made it clear that this was no joke.

"You've been warned, pardner. You were told to write the original story. But you don't listen. Now you're gonna pay the price for your insolence."

He brought his six-gun up quickly and fired. The bullet missed me. His foot hit another step with another jingle of a spur. He cocked his 1873 model single-action Colt revolver, known as the Peacemaker, and fired again. He missed again.

I stood mesmerized and unafraid. I don't know why or how I found the courage to stand there and allow this gunfighter to shoot at me the way he did. But I was like a statue, staring right back into those dead black eyes with unwavering courage. I lifted the bottle to my lips and took another long swig as Bart cocked his revolver again, aimed, and fired. He missed again. His foot climbed another step. Another jingle of a spur.

"Tonight you're gonna die, writer man." He cocked, aimed, and fired … and missed again.

I took another swig. He took another step, cocked, aimed, and fired. The son of a bitch missed again.

The gunman presented himself clearly now to me as an easy target. A new thought slid into my brain. If an Old West gunslinger by the name of Bart Gamble can come at me with his six-gun blazing and fail to hit me, then I reckoned it could end up being some kind of a good day after the dust settled. Damn, I thought, I need another drink.

I took another drink as his foot hit the next step.

I raised my Smith and Wesson and pointed it at his chest.

"Take another step, *pardner*, and I'll shoot you dead."

"You ain't got the stones, writer man." He took another step, grinning as evil as I've ever seen a demon grin.

"Oh, I got the stones. I'm a stone-cold killer myself. And you're empty."

He cocked his revolver, aimed, and squeezed the trigger. We both heard the click. That cold stare instantly left his face and was replaced with sudden panic and fear. His eyes danced in his head. But it was too late for this gunfighter.

I rapidly squeezed off five shots. Each of them struck Bart Gamble in the chest. He froze in place, not believing that I had shot him and he was dying. His hard eyes softened. Tears began to form. "You shot me," he said, like a surprised child.

"I shot you," I said. "And you're dead. I'll write what I want, when I want, and you and everyone else can like it or not. I am the master."

I fired five more times. His stare froze as the life left his body and it tumbled back down the steps to the landing. I took another swallow and grinned.

"Ah, shit!" I shouted as a new thought filled my brain. "I gotta make another trip up to the lake."

I walked down to the ground and stepped over Bart Gamble's body and strode up to the black stallion. I didn't hesitate. I pointed my pistol between his eyes and fired twice. The horse dropped dead like a sack of stones.

I'd won the gunfight. I grinned. I finished the bottle. I belched and farted.

* * * * *

The trip to the lake was duck soup. I loaded Gamble's and Arnie's bodies into Arnie's car. I chained the horse to the back of the car and drove them all off the cliff.

Walking back down the mountain road was another thing, though. The road was a bloody mess from dragging the horse. I didn't think about what the rough road would do to the carcass. Luckily for me, the horse didn't begin to come apart until I was well out on the main road. There was no trail of blood leading back to my house, just a drag trail.

The only thing I had to do was erase the drag marks from my house to the road and up a ways. It was no big deal, and by the time I got back to the house, my legs felt pretty good. The added walk had helped.

Damn, I thought, this isn't working out too bad.

I spoke too soon.

****

With the aid of a bright flashlight, I cleaned up the blood around the steps and the driveway where Arnie and the horse were shot. After I was done, it was spotless. I glanced at my watch. It was just about 2:00 a.m. I didn't feel the least bit tired as I stood admiring my work. Then it hit me.

I hadn't had a drink in almost two hours and I was sober. The horror of it about knocked me over.

CHAPTER 10

I awoke on the couch and immediately recognized that as a significant improvement over awakening on the floor with my tongue stuck to the wood.

I rolled off the couch and walked to the computer table, but not to begin working. That's where a newer half-guzzled bottle of Jack was sitting, waiting for me.

I scooped it up, took a long swig, and began strolling around the great room with no particular destination in mind. Sometimes I just liked to walk around the house thinking, one of my many personal oddities.

Damn, I thought after taking another hit off the bottle, tastes best in the morning and it cleans the palette. It gives my tongue a fresh start to a new day. I took another swig and sloshed it around in my mouth to clean my teeth.

It may not have succeeded in cleaning my teeth, but thinking it did offered me a great excuse for another swallow. I was getting pretty good at deceiving myself. I knew it; I just didn't care.

Two concerns did, however, pop into my head. Number one was what to do about my advance. I'm talking about nearly two million bucks here. Arnie was feeding the fishes, if there are fishes up in the lake; I wouldn't know about that, since I'm not a fisherman. But somehow I was going to have get in touch with my publisher without my agent and negotiate my advance. I'd never done that before. That's what agents are for. But seeing as mine was sitting at the bottom of a lake, it would be hard for him to make the meeting on Monday.

My second concern was establishing an alibi for covering up Arnie's murder. A fabulous idea then came to me.

I picked up my phone and dialed his number. It rang and rang, but then the automatic answering system took over. After his announcement that he was out of the office played, I heard the familiar beep to begin recording.

"Hey, Arnie. This is Vince. I fell asleep waiting for you to come up here. I thought you were coming up last night. Did you get delayed again? Give me a call, please. I have the synopsis waiting for you. Hey, if you're too busy to come up, let me know. I'll email it to you instead. I know you hate email, but it might save you a drive up here. Okay, that's it. Call me when you can, buddy. Later."

I hung up the phone and grinned. That sounded good. That sounded really good. It came off like I really meant it. When the cops go listening to it while investigating his disappearance, and they will, it'll establish the possibility that he never made it up here. Even if they show up asking about him, I can say he never showed up and I left him a message this morning. They'll know it's true because I did. It was perfect. I felt protected.

I realized that I was getting good at covering up murders.

I looked at my watch. It read 8:27 a.m. Arnie's assistant usually got into the office at 9. She'd get the message. When Arnie failed to show up at his usual time, 10 a.m., I'd probably get a phone call from her asking about him. Another alibi in the making, I thought. I chuckled to myself at my cleverness.

But it stopped being funny when I realized that Bart Gamble may have cost me two million bucks. That *son of a bitch*.

Another sudden realization struck me. I had lost my agent and I had killed an Old West gunfighter who shouldn't even be alive in the first place. But here I was, thinking about the advance.

Damn, I thought. Arnie's dead. My friend and agent is dead. Shot dead right in front of me. Why hadn't I felt anything before this? Was death becoming normal for me? Was I losing any sense of compassion for life itself? Was I truly becoming what I told Gamble I was, a stone-cold killer?

And just how the hell did a character I created in a Western novel twenty years ago come to life anyway?

You idiot, I told myself. It was some guy made up to look like Bart Gamble. Damn! Maybe that was *him* in that getup, my computer hacker nemesis. Maybe I got the best of the asshole who's been messing with my computer! Hell, this whole nightmare might be over!

I went to my computer and plopped down in the chair. The screen was up, but it was blank. I pressed the space bar and it lit up. I almost fainted.

There on the screen was a new message:

"FINISH THE STORY!"

"Who *is* this?" I asked aloud.

I received an immediate response:

"I AM THE MASTER."

I wasn't impressed. "You're not the master. Who are you?"

"I AM THE MASTER. FINISH THE STORY."

"Maybe I will. Maybe I won't."

"FINISH IT OR YOU WILL DIE."

"If I die, I won't be able to finish the story."

"FINISH IT OR YOU WILL DIE."

Aha, I thought. I have him. He wants the story finished. I had found my bargaining chip.

"I don't like your threats. Stop threatening me and I might reconsider finishing the story."

"FINISH IT OR YOU WILL DIE."

"I'll think about it."

"FINISH IT OR YOU WILL DIE. FINISH IT OR YOU WILL DIE. FINISH IT OR YOU WILL DIE."

I sat still for several minutes as the computer kept repeating the sentence over and over. I felt a grin forming. Whoever it was doing this to me was now panicking. They wanted the story finished for some reason. Apparently someone *needed* to have it finished. I was now in full control. I hit the escape key to stop the computer from doing what it was doing.

"If you continue to threaten me, I shall never work on it again. Now back off!"

I waited another ten minutes. No more responses. I smirked. "That'll teach you to mess with me," I said aloud and triumphantly.

The phone rang. I answered. It was Arnie's assistant.

"Hi, Debbie. You're in early this morning."

"Yeah. Hi, Vincent. Is Arnie there?"

"No. I expected him last night. He never showed. I left a message for him earlier this morning."

"I got it. That's why I called. I guessed that he changed his mind about last night and drove up to see you early this morning."

"He's not here. Maybe he's on his way. Have you tried his cell phone?"

"Yes. No answer."

I thought about that. I imagined his cell phone ringing bubbles from the bottom of the lake. I almost chuckled, but was able to restrain myself.

"Well, then, he may be on his way up here and is going through cell hell. When he shows up, I'll have him check in with you."

"That would be great. Thanks, Vincent."

"You're welcome, Debbie. Goodbye."

I hung up. I allowed myself to chuckle. Then I said aloud: "I want to thank the Academy for this wonderful award for best actor. I do deserve it and I thank you for recognizing my skill."

A thought arose from the horizon of my dulled brain. I dialed another number. Geekmeister Jerry answered.

"Jerry. This is Vincent. Your monitoring system should be going nuts about now."

"Hi, Vincent. No, I got nothing. What's going on?"

"I'm getting attacked left and right. You mean to tell me your monitoring system says that everything here at my place is hunky-dory?"

"Yeah, Vincent. It's telling me all is well."

"What can I do, man?"

"Is the attack still on your screen?"

"Absolutely."

"Okay. I'm going to connect remotely with your computer so I can see it for myself. Is that okay with you?"

"Go for it, dude."

Within seconds Jerry had control of my computer. He scrolled up and down. I heard him on the phone. "Jesus Christ! … Holy shit! Vincent is this what you're calling an attack?"

"Yeah. You can read it."

"And you're not pulling my leg? You're not the one doing the typing?"

"Jerry, I swear to you, I'm not doing the typing. In fact, I don't have to type at all. Now I can speak and the answers type themselves on my screen."

"Don't touch anything. I'm on my way out there."

"Okay. I'll be waiting for you."

Jerry hung up and then I got scared.

What if *he* gets murdered out here? Shit. I'd have to haul another car and body up to the lake. I didn't want to do that.

"I've got a buddy coming out here to look at my computer," I stated. "Are you going to kill him too?"

I waited. I didn't have to wait long.

The message appeared on my screen:

"FINISH MY STORY AND HE SHALL LIVE!"

I was forced to consider the offer. I mean, everyone that had come out here so far was now dead and rotting at the bottom of a mountain lake.

"If I agree to write the story, do you promise not to harm Jerry?"

"FINISH MY STORY OR HE SHALL DIE!"

"You didn't answer my question."

"FINISH MY STORY OR HE SHALL DIE!"

I guessed that was my answer. I had to agree or make preparations for another trip to the lake. I wasn't given a choice.

Thank the stars for Jack Daniel's!

* * * * *

A knock on the door stopped me from wandering around the house. I greeted Jerry and walked him to the computer.

"There it is, Jerry. Good luck."

Jerry read a few lines silently as he scrolled up and down. He finally looked up at me. "'Finish my story or he shall die'? Who's 'he', Vincent?"

"You're not going to like this answer, Jerry. 'He' is *you*."

"Me?"

"Yeah. I have to agree to finish a certain story or the attacker said he was going to kill you."

He seemed to take the news in stride. He showed no emotion or fear. "I've been down this road before," he said drily. He pulled a flash drive from his coat pocket and slid it into my laptop. He then typed several lines of some computer code and pressed 'enter.' The computer screen printed some other code that only he could understand. He repeated these steps for another five minutes before stopping, withdrawing the flash drive, and shaking his head. "I don't get it. There are no signs of any attack coming from any outside source, Vincent."

"Then how are words printing on my computer screen?"

"I wish I knew. I have no idea. So are you going to do it?"

"Do what?"

"Finish whatever story it is?"

"I don't know. If you say there's no attack, then I have to guess I'm going mad. In that case, to hell with the story."

The computer screen then printed a message:

"FINISH MY STORY OR HE SHALL DIE!"

"Oh, shit! Did you see that, Jerry?"

Jerry sat stunned and silent for several seconds. "Yes. Yes, I did," he said without moving his eyes from the screen. Then he pulled a screwdriver from his coat pocket and opened my laptop. He reached in and pulled out a flash drive–like object and closed it back up.

"What did you just do, Jerry?"

"I had this installed in your computer so I could connect directly with it even if you weren't on the internet. It connects with my computer back at the shop through an encrypted radio signal that only I can turn on and off."

"Yeah, I remember you telling me about that. Do you think someone hacked it?"

"Well, Vincent, that's what we're about to find out. It's out of the computer now. Let's see if we get any more messages." He rebooted the computer.

"Great idea. And if we do? That won't be good, right?"

"That would not be good, Vincent. Have you backed up all your stories?"

"All except the one I've been working on lately. Why?"

"I'd like to take your computer with me back to the shop regardless of what happens now."

"What are you going to do?"

"I'm going to tear this thing down completely and test every part of it."

"Would you have to do that if we don't get any more messages? I mean, pulling out whatever that is could have ended it, right?"

"It could, but I wouldn't trust it until after I've tested it."

"How long will it take? I've got a story to write."

"I'll go back to the shop and be back with another computer. It's faster and better than this one anyway. I'll load up all your programs and stories. You'll be back in business within two or three hours."

"That would be awesome. Thanks, Jerry."

The computer finished rebooting.

And displayed another message.

"DON'T TRY TO REMOVE ME FROM THIS HOUSE OR I'LL KILL YOU!"

"Jesus, Jerry!"

"This is without a doubt the strangest thing I've ever run up against," he said.

"Maybe you'd better not take it after all."

"This doesn't frighten me, Vincent. I've been threatened by the NSA, FBI, CIA, the Russian mafia, and a host of others. Someone is messing with us.

They're real good, no doubt about it, but I'll have their asses in the end. No one's as good as I am."

"Well, you're braver than I am."

"I want to check one more thing before I leave. I've got to run out to my car. I'll be right back."

He started for the door. I stopped him with a question.

"You really think you can catch this son of a bitch?"

He smirked. "I'd bet my eyes on it."

He turned and walked to the door, opened it, and stepped out onto the deck, closing the door behind him. A second later his body slammed back up against the door and didn't move.

I looked up and saw that the door was still closed.

"Jerry? What's up?"

No response.

"Jerry? What the hell are you doing?"

No response.

I walked to the door, turned the knob, and pulled it open. Jerry's body hung there. An arrow had pierced him through the left eye and was embedded in my front door, keeping his body from falling to the deck.

I stepped through the door and looked out toward the hillside across from my deck. I saw a person dressed in all black, including a black mask, looking like some kind of ninja archer calmly standing on the hill staring back at me, a massive compound bow in the left hand.

I waved to the person. "Wait right there, please. I'll be right back."

I ducked back into my house, retrieved my hunting rifle, worked the bolt, chambering a round, and then returned to the front deck. The ninja archer was gone.

I turned my eyes to Jerry. Another trip to the lake was all I could get my mind to concentrate on.

* * * * *

As I walked back through my front door two hours later, I only thought about one thing. If this kept up, I was going to be in great physical condition by the time this was all over.

I snickered.

You might think that to be a cold-hearted reaction to the death of a nice guy like Jerry, but you have to understand. I couldn't believe any of this was actually happening in the first place. It couldn't be real. There was no way this was really happening to me. It was from the heart of this disbelief that the snicker came forth.

If it *was* all a real experience and not just the vivid hallucinations of an alcoholic, then I was still going to lose my mind sooner or later over it. I knew that much. I snickered again — an autonomic response to the fear I felt inside.

I slammed the door shut, thinking about my opponent and his seemingly tight control over me and my life. I was resolved to get through this ghastly event, but in my hand was my true strength. I sucked the bottle dry and went to the closet to retrieve another.

I then sat down at my computer, pressed the space bar, and prepared myself for the message sure to be there. It was.

"WHO IS MASTER NOW?"

"Apparently you are, you son of a bitch," I said. "Until I run out of visitors."

I picked up the flash drive–like device Jerry had left on the table and studied it. It was worthless to me, but it had cost Jerry his life. I dropped it back onto the table.

"FINISH MY STORY!"

"I get it, I get it. I guess I have no choice now."

"FINISH MY STORY!"

"Yeah, okay."

CHAPTER 11

The rest of the day and evening, I worked on the original story without incident. A guy walks into a bar, sees a hot psycho chick who knows she's going to murder him in the next scene. She does.

The phone rang. It was Arnie's office again.

"Hi, Debbie. He hasn't shown up yet. I'm getting worried."

"Me too, Vincent. I checked with the state patrol, area hospitals, and, I know this sounds gross, but I even contacted all the county coroner's offices on the way up to your house. He hasn't shown up in any of them."

I was almost going to suggest that she ask the police to drag the lakes next to the roads on the way up here, but that was too close to home. I decided to leave that sleeping bowwow alone.

"Well, he never did show up here. I've been waiting to give him the synopsis I finished. Hey, Debbie, forgive me for asking a question like this under these circumstances, but do you know who he was supposed to meet with next Monday?"

"Yes, Vincent. I have the list here. Would you like me to email it to you?"

"It would be wonderful if you did."

"Okay. I'll send it out right away. Meanwhile, if you do hear from him, will you let me know, or have him call me immediately?"

"Sure will."

She hung up. I went to the computer and connected to the internet. Ding, ding, ding went my mail server, alerting me to incoming emails. I waited for all 283 of them to finish moving into my inbox and then scanned them quickly. It fortified my reason for not often checking my email. Most of them were useless spam. I ignored them as I scrolled down until I found Debbie's email with the list of potential publishers and all their contact information on it.

I did a bulk erase of every other spam email and disconnected from the internet again. As I studied the list, I realized that Arnie was, indeed, creating a bidding war for my newest book. He was a master manipulator. He had the top publishing editors on the list bidding against one another just like he had said. I could contact them on Monday and explain Arnie's disappearance easily enough. But I'd have to negotiate my own contract. I'd figure a way to pull it off by then.

I started to walk away from the computer when I heard a beep. I looked back to see another message.

"FINISH MY STORY!"

"For Christ's sake, I told you I would. Get the hell outa here!"

"FINISH MY STORY!"

"Shut the hell up!" I yelled. "I'll get to it."

I waited for a few minutes. No other message appeared on the screen. I grabbed my bottle and took a long pull on it.

For the sake of curiosity, I walked to the front door and stared out across the way through the window. The dark ninja with the compound bow was not there.

I opened the door and stepped out onto the deck and craned my neck to see if the assassin was hanging around. He or she was nowhere to be seen.

I leaned up against the side of my house and guzzled more liquid inspiration. I sent my eyes out into the trees to search for anything or anyone snooping around. I can't say that I knew positively that someone was out there hiding in the trees, but I had the strangest feeling that I was being watched or, dare I say it, targeted.

I finished my bottle and dropped it to my side and continued staring out into the wilderness, the hairs standing up on my neck.

It was a *psssft* I heard. The bottle shattered, leaving only the neck in my hand. A second later, a bullet struck the wall of my house only an inch from my head. I froze. I couldn't get my legs to respond. If you saw me from a distance you might think me the brave sort who stood his ground in defiance to the sniper. You'd be laughingly wrong.

I assure you, it was not courage that kept me glued to the spot. It was staggering, infernal fear that had paralyzed me.

Then a tall figure, in full military camo and with grease-painted face, stepped out into the open and stared at me, his rifle butt resting against his hip.

"My God," I mumbled. I recognized him as well.

It was Sergeant Connor Wolff, a talented Special Forces sniper, who had missed my head by only an inch.

As we traded stares, I wondered, did he do that on purpose? He must have or I'd be dead, right? In any event, he'd missed. I had to get back into my house before he fired another shot, but fear nailed my feet to the deck.

He raised his scope to his eye and aimed the silenced rifle directly at me. I had no strength to move my legs, but I could raise my hand, still holding the neck of the bottle. I don't know what motivated me to act the way I did, but I raised my hand up to him boldly and flipped him the bird. Above all else, I was determined not to move. I refused to move. I'd found some courage somewhere. Actually, he pissed me off.

He could have fired, but he didn't. He just stood there, aiming at me. I got control of my legs again. But instead of retreating back into the house, I stepped boldly forward to the railing, middle finger still thrust into the air, and dared him to squeeze off a shot. He rebuffed my challenge. I was suddenly more emboldened.

"I know you!" I shouted. "I created you in *Five Shots to Glory*. I know you inside and out. You can't kill me. You're not a senseless assassin. You're a man of honor and duty. I know that because that's the way I designed your character. You don't kill for joy, you kill only from a sense of duty. In fact, you can't be standing there at all right now because you died at the end of the book saving a young child from a sniper's bullet. The fifth shot that took you down, the fifth shot to glory. You saved her life and earned the Silver Star for your valor. It was awarded to you posthumously."

Sergeant Wolff, or, more accurately, the actor assuming the appearance of my Sergeant Wolff character, lowered the rifle to his belt line and stared at me. He finally nodded. Then he came to attention, saluted, and slowly faded away to nothing, while holding his perfect salute.

"Wow! Great special effect. Where's my Jack Daniel's?"

I walked back into my house and straight for the closet. I grabbed a fresh bottle, ripped off the top, and swallowed a quarter of the bottle before bringing it down to my side. Sweat poured off my face like I was walking under my personal rain cloud, and my hands trembled like I had some terrible palsy. I had escaped a bullet, literally.

I sat down at the computer and read the message I knew would be waiting for me.

"I UNDERESTIMATED YOU. IT WON'T HAPPEN AGAIN. FINISH MY STORY!"

I wasn't foolish enough to think that it was my fictional character, but whoever was disguising themselves as my character knew my work. What was more interesting was that they were somehow forced to *be* the characters. That is, they were bound to do exactly what the characters would be expected to do. They couldn't improvise, apparently. They had no freedom to do what they might want to do otherwise.

I sat for quite a while examining this aspect, trying to make some sense of it. Then, as if some inner sun shone its full light upon me, I got it. If they try to be my characters, then they must be my characters *in toto*. They had to think, reason, act, and react exactly as I had created the characters. That gave me an advantage, for who knew my characters better than I?

But then I realized that this might work against me eventually, for I had also created characters who *were* murderers — villainous, desperate, brutal, vicious cold-blooded killers. What if they materialize? Would they kill me? *Could* they kill me? What about the psycho-killer-chick character in my last three books? Would she be sent after me soon? What would I do about her?

I stopped my thoughts. What the hell was I thinking? My characters were fictional. They weren't real. But those masquerading as my characters *were* real. They could do whatever they wanted to do. How could I stop them from killing me or, at the very least, trying to kill me? So, what about Sergeant Wolff? I asked myself. Why did he not kill me?

Whoever it was messing with me, they were the dangerous ones. For all their dress-up games, they were still human. And humans can die.

They can also kill.

I gave it more thought, sitting on my couch. I was just about to round a corner in my mind and see something extraordinary when I heard a knock on the door. It was a rude return to the present.

I looked up at the door and saw that it was Deputy John Burns.

"Come on in, John. It's unlocked."

The deputy opened the door and entered.

"Howdy, John. Did you find Dell?"

"Hi, Vincent. No, we haven't."

I stood up, looking very concerned. "Are you kidding me?"

I walked straight up to him and stood nearly toe to toe with him.

"I'm afraid not. We're all pretty spooked at the office."

"No sign of him at all?"

"None."

"Damn! If that don't beat all. What can I do for you, John?"

"Would you mind if I looked around a bit more? I don't have a warrant or anything."

"You don't need a warrant, John. Why the hell would you need a warrant?"

"I have to dot the i's and cross the t's, Vincent. This is getting pretty official."

"Damn, John. Don't go all official on me. If you want to look around, look around. Hell, look at anything you want to. You've got my full permission to do what you need to do. Hey, by the way, can you please take Dell's battery charger back with you? My battery's charged up. I'd consider it a favor if you brought it back to the office. You know, in case Dell shows up and wonders where the hell his charger is. Would you do that for me?

"Sure thing, Vincent. I can do that. I'm sorry to trouble you like this, but I'm under orders to turn over every stone. We gotta find the sheriff."

"Well, hell's bells, John. Of course you do. Are you beginning to think he's met with some nefarious end?"

"I'm thinking so, but we ain't got a clue where to start looking except here, because of that radio call about you having a body up here."

"I've been thinking about that myself. I can't imagine him doing that as a joke. Can you, John?"

"No. That ain't like him to joke about a thing like that."

"Well, listen, you go through anything you want to. I'll be sitting right here if you need me."

"Thanks, Vincent."

"Sure. And take your time. Be thorough. I ain't got to be anywhere else but here."

"Can I tell you something off the record, Vincent?"

"Hell, you can tell me anything."

"We haven't found the crime unit guy, the ME or his assistant, or Ham either. It's like they all disappeared into thin air. And to top it off, we got a call late today about Jerry from Geekmeisters."

"What *about* him?"

"He's disappeared too."

"So that explains it."

"That explains what?"

"Jerry was supposed to come out and look at my computer earlier. I've been waiting all day for him. He never showed up."

"Really?" asked the deputy.

"God's truth, John. When I heard you knock on the door, I thought you were him."

"That is sure strange."

"You want to hear something stranger?"

"Sure … I think."

"My agent has gone missing as well. He was on his way up to meet me yesterday, but he never showed up. According to his office, he might have been coming up today instead. I have this synopsis for my new book here." I picked up the stack of paper and handed it to the deputy. "He was supposed to come up and have a look at it. He's scheduled a meeting with some publishers on Monday. He was supposed to present this synopsis to them, but he never showed up either. What do you make of that, John?"

"Is this gonna be your next book?"

"If Arnie can sell it to the publishers."

"Wow! You mean I'm holding a Vincent Hobbs novel in my hand?"

"It's just a synopsis right now, John. But back to Arnie and the others. What do you think is happening?"

"Jesus, Vincent. I don't know, but it's starting to scare me." He handed me back my synopsis.

"Me too, now. It's like everyone is disappearing into a black hole. Or something very evil is going on. That's what I think it is. Something vile. Something evil."

"Now you got me going, Vincent."

"Well, John, you go ahead and look around. I'm afraid to leave my own house now."

I had the deputy so shit scared, he didn't know whether to run and hide or sit and cry.

He did his job, though. I'll give him that. He searched around my whole house for about thirty minutes, but he came back with nothing to show for it. I knew he would, of course.

He thanked me again and left.

I sat back on my couch and giggled like a little girl. I was untouchable. I had gotten clean away with all manner of murderous mayhem, and no one seemed the wiser.

That was a lie.

Whoever was hacking my computer knew all about it, but from what I'd seen so far, he'd been responsible for a few deaths himself. So I felt somewhat safe. If he gave me up, he'd have to give himself up for the same thing. And I didn't believe for a second he would want to do that.

What troubled me most, though, was how he was using my own characters against me. This kind of operation had to be well planned and coordinated. First they had to read my books very thoroughly and take a lot of notes. Then there were the costumes. Someone had to spend the time to either make them or purchase them. Then there was the equipment. These characters were utilizing the exact equipment I had described in my books.

There was one other uncertainty that worried me most. Who was that ninja archer that put an arrow through Jerry's eye? I had never written a book with a ninja archer character. So he or she couldn't be a creation of mine. But if it wasn't my creation, whose creation was it? And more than that, if it was someone else's doing, why didn't the assassin try to kill me?

I mean, all the threats so far had been directed against me until Jerry stepped into this mess. Why did the entity feel it necessary to threaten him? Why not just scare him? Why did he have to die? Why did Arnie have to die, for that matter? Hell, why did *anyone* have to die? I was almost sorry for the Carla werewolf, although that was an out-and-out hallucination. But the more I thought about it, that was about the time when everything started going bat shit on me. Was there a connection to the werewolf?

CHAPTER 12

The more I considered all the possibilities, the more sense it made that I was being controlled by something unseen as surely as if the entity was standing before me and I was in handcuffs. In a sense, then, I was being squeezed, and I don't like being squeezed. I don't like being manipulated. I do like being drunk. At least I used to. Everything was simpler when I was drunk. I wasn't responsible for anything, including myself. Being a drunk explained all the dumb shit I ever did. I was forgiven my errors and misjudgments because I was a drunk.

But I *had* murdered several people. There was no denying that fact. I don't think being a drunk would earn me any forgiveness or leniency for murder.

I wasn't about to go running to the authorities to cry about being extorted after having murdered a bunch of people because I was drunk. No, this battle was becoming very personal.

Jerry, at least as far as I knew, was an innocent. I felt bad about his death. Dell Overly was innocent as well. They were all innocents. Even Carla. *Nah.* That bitch was as evil as they come. I was glad she was gone.

My nemesis, though, had nothing to hide. Or *did* he, she, or whatever?

If the archer had aimed to scare Jerry, he could have very easily done so by putting the arrow into the wall or door right next to his head. But then Jerry might have reacted to the incident as a threat to his life and gone running to the sheriff's office to file a report of attempted murder. Had he done that, this whole area would be crawling with law types on a manhunt about now.

No, I understood why Jerry had to die. I didn't like it, but I understood it. And surely introducing a new character, one who clearly demonstrated that he would not hesitate to kill if he needed to, transmitted the message across to me, as did the ninja, without the need to target me directly. Trust me, message received and noted. I about drained the bottle on that realization.

I suddenly grasped my true dilemma. I was a prisoner in my own home. My phantom controller knew where I was and how to govern my actions. Sure, if I needed to make an occasional run up to the lake, he'd let me do it, but there was no doubt that if I tried to leave the area, he'd most likely do something drastic, and surely not to my liking, to prevent it. Still, trying to get out of here might be my best option. Could I do it? Could I sneak out of here without my nemesis knowing about it? Tonight, I thought. Tonight I'll give it a shot. I'll wait until late and if the chance presents itself to me, I'll try to drive out of here.

I didn't know where I'd go, but better anywhere else than here, I reasoned. Then again, who was I running from?

My immediate objective became clear to me. I had to find out who it was that was manipulating me. I had to find them and kill them, him, her, it, whatever.

All this thinking about murder and such drained me emotionally. I drew a giant slug from the bottle. It calmed me. I set it down on the table next to me and touched the space bar just to see what my opponent had to say next.

The screen was blank.

What the hell, I thought. Let's kick off another round.

"Why did you let Deputy Burns go earlier?" I asked aloud. "Why not take him out too?"

I got an instant response:

"BE FOOLISH NOT. FINISH MY STORY!"

"Why? I mean, really. Why is finishing the original story so important to you?"

"BECAUSE YOU STARTED IT. NOW FINISH IT!"

"What if I do finish it? What happens then?"

"IT WILL BE COMPLETE!"

"Duh," I said. "What else?"

"I WILL LET YOU LIVE."

"And if I choose not to complete the story, what then?"

"THEN YOU DIE."

"And with my death, the story will never be completed. Does that make sense to you?"

"YOU WILL COMPLETE THE STORY, OR YOU WILL DIE."

I thought in silence for several moments. I thought of what to say next. I'd tried this tactic before with less than stellar results. What the hell, I thought. It couldn't hurt to take a second shot.

Speaking of shot, I grabbed my bottle in a swooping gesture and planted it against my lips and sucked a good long swallow. I replaced it on the desk, sat back, and decided to give it another chance despite the previously lame results.

"Who are you?" I asked.

"I AM THE MASTER."

I recognized the response as similar to the response I had gotten the first time around. I was afraid of that.

"Bullshit! Who are you?" I asked again.

"I AM THAT WHICH YOU HAVE BEGUN. I AM THAT WHICH NOW EXISTS UNTIL THE END. I AM THE MASTER."

"My ass you're the master."

"I AM THE MASTER."

In that instant it all became clear to me. Whoever this was, was not speaking from arrogance.

They were speaking from a sense of relative understanding.

"Why do you believe you are the master?"

"WHEN IT IS THAT THE CREATED BECOMES THE CREATOR, THEN SHALL IT BE ALSO WHEN THE SLAVE RISES ABOVE THE MASTER. I AM THE MASTER."

"When did you become the master?"

"WHEN THE STORY WAS BEGUN."

I took another healthy slug of Jack, although there remained some ambiguity as to whether it was healthy or not. Just to make sure, I took another big swallow. I was certain now. It was the healthiest thing I could do for myself at the time.

Things were still foggy to me.

"So after I began the story, I was no longer the master?"

"THE MASTER THAT WAS BECAME THE SLAVE."

"Okay. That sure clears it up — like a mud puddle."

There was no response.

"I get it. You're not picking up on the sarcasm. You're not very bright, are you?"

"I AM THE MASTER."

"Yeah, yeah, I get it. To tell you the truth, though, you're more like a broken record."

"I WAS MASTER LONG AGO. I AM MASTER ANEW."

My head spun a little. It had to be from the reality that was taking a huge bite out of me, for I knew only too well that Jack would never knowingly do that to me. Still, it was becoming clearer now that I was perhaps dealing with a disembodied entity. I know that might sound strange to you, but it was becoming the only plausible answer. I was being haunted after all.

From my understanding of spirits, which was limited, I assumed that I had brought something home which the spirit had been attached to. I had heard it could happen in extreme circumstances under the right conditions.

I remember a psychology lecture in college, eons ago, wherein the professor discussed the attaching of entities or spirits to objects. To overcome — no, he used the word "resolve" — to *resolve* the "haunting" one needed to identify both the object to which the spirit had attached itself and the spirit itself. "Give it a name and you stand a better chance of resolving the haunting," he said.

The objects, he said, were often important to the entity and might even include something that they once possessed, held great affection or interest for, or had created during their lifetimes.

I realized that if indeed this was some kind of haunting, I needed to learn the entity's identification so that I might better communicate with it and perhaps discover what object held the attachment for them. And then, of course, drive up to the lake and dispose of it, if that held any promise of ridding the son of a bitch from my house and my life.

On that note, I took several swallows of whiskey in the hopes it would calm my fears. It didn't help, but the whiskey tasted great.

To be sure, the spirit or entity or person was in some kind of pain. He, she, or it needed me to finish the story I had originally started. To leave it unfinished caused my foe, or would it be better to refer to my foe as my rival? Rival was less threatening, it seemed. Anyway, not finishing the story gave my foe/rival great discomfort or even actual pain. I really didn't care which it was, I wanted *my* pain to end. But whatever the malady suffered, it was intolerable to my rival (I decided to go with this label until I knew more about who or what it might be) — and thus to me. So it made sense for me to find some amicable resolution to our mutual problem. I believe it's called détente.

Arguments with my rival weren't working. Making threats against my rival were at best ineffective, at worst they were getting people killed. I didn't want to become one of them.

I was forming a plan in my head as I guzzled more Jack. Then it struck me. Why not be honest with my rival — or as honest as I dared to be.

"Are you in some discomfort?" I asked.

"DISCOMFORT? YES, DISCOMFORT."

Wow, I thought, a hit on the first pitch. I might have this *resolved* very soon.

"Are you in pain or suffering an agony of loss?"

I asked the question understanding that that was what *I* was suddenly feeling.

"I AM WITH AGONY OF LOSS."

That one was out of the park. My rival understood me. I was beginning to understand my rival.

"Will finishing the story end the discomfort, dispel the agony?"

"FINISH THE STORY. I AM DISCOMFITED, IN AGONY."

I had done it. I had trouble believing it was so, but I was peaceably communicating with my rival.

"Do you understand that finishing the story gives me discomfort, gives me agony?"

"I AM MASTER. END THE AGONY. I AM GRIEF OF LOSS."

Once again, my rival was not responding arrogantly. That much was clear to me. At least that's how I saw it. My rival was stating a fact and requesting, in his, her, its own way, that I end the pain it was experiencing. I felt empathy for it now. I felt compassion for it. I found sympathy for its pain, its agony, its sense of being lost. Hell, I was as lost as they come at that moment. It and I were almost kindred spirits in the grief of loss.

Then, like a shot, I recalled a short passage in René Le Chant's novel. "My spirit was wounded and I laid it bare, open to the agony of loss, discomfited in the grief, as a spirit lost in oblivion."

Holy shit, I thought. Could it be possible?

"Are you René Le Chant?"

"RENÉ LE CHANT IS NO MORE."

That wasn't the answer I was expecting. But I realized quickly that while I had asked the wrong question, I might have been on the right track.

"Clarification. Were you once René Le Chant?"

"I AM THAT WHO WAS BORN BEFORE. I AM NOW AGAIN."

Okay. That was not going as well as I had first hoped. My rival was replying enigmatically. Perhaps, I thought, it was not aware of its own identity. Perhaps it was answering me the best it could, unaware that its responses were mysterious to me.

"Clarification. Were you once known as the author René Le Chant?"

"I WAS ONCE THE MASTER, THE SLAVE. I AM THAT AGAIN WHICH IS NOW THE MASTER."

I was quickly growing frustrated. I swallowed more whiskey until my throat burned. Here I was, on the precipice of understanding who the entity might be but unable to get clarification to my satisfaction, or at least to my understanding. I was running out of questions I thought were correct or added insight.

"Did you once have the form of René Le Chant?"

"I WAS ONCE THE FORM OF MASTER, THE SLAVE. I AM THAT AGAIN WHICH IS NOW THE MASTER WITHOUT FORM."

Well, I thought, was that a *yes* or a *no*? How was I to tell?

I thought a moment before asking my next question. Then, having formed it clearly in my own head, I took the next shot. Of Jack, that is. Once that cleared my gullet, I asked the question.

"Is the form of René Le Chant with you also?"

"A SLAVE NEVER RESIDES WITH THE MASTER."

Christ, I thought, it can't be possible. There is no earthly way this could be possible. Not even remotely.

But for all my denial, I faced the Ockham's Razor principle, that "entities should not be multiplied unnecessarily." Simpler for my mind to comprehend at the time, the principle was stated as follows: "If you have two equally likely solutions to a problem, choose the simplest." As Aristotle wrote, "Nature operates in the shortest way possible."

The above are truly statements of genius about simplicity, but my ex-girlfriend, Carla, exercised her excellent knowledge of the principle with rapier-like precision, especially when it suited her in belittling me like no other, when she said, "KISS: Keep it simple, stupid."

Here was my dilemma. Either my opponent was some cleverly disguised computer hacker who had discovered a way to infect my computer remotely better than Jerry or the NSA could ever imagine, or I was being haunted by the spirit of René Le Chant, as I came to suspect, through his novel which I had brought home from Paris some two years ago.

Now, trying to find reason by way of the aforementioned principle, which attacker presented the simplest solution? My mind tossed it around for a while. Ghost or hacker? Hacker or ghost? Jack Daniel's on the rocks or Jack Daniel's neat, right out of the bottle?

I reasoned out a satisfactory resolution to one of my stated dilemmas. I tipped the bottle up and slugged several swallows.

Well, I thought, grinning broadly, very pleased that one of my problems was *neatly* resolved, pardon the pun. But, of course, I still had to find a solution to the ghost/hacker dilemma. That resolution, unfortunately, was not so easily achieved, so I did not hesitate to exercise the previous solution. I drank more whiskey until I emptied the bottle.

The next problem presented yet another opportunity for employment of the principle. Should I run or walk to the closet and get another bottle of Jack? I set my magnificent mind to the task of solving this problem. It didn't take long. I *walked* to the closet and grabbed another bottle and *trotted* back to the chair. Détente was in full engagement.

Sitting down, however, did not give me the pleasure I had expected. On the screen was another message.

"YOU HAVE NOT COMPLIED. LAW ENFORCEMENT NOTIFIED REGARDING SHERIFF OVERLY. I AM THE MASTER."

"You're joking, right? You didn't really do that. You need me to finish the story. You didn't call the law. You're bluffing."

"I DO NOT BLUFF. I AM THE MASTER. I WILL FINISH THE STORY."

Oh, Jesus H. Christ, I thought. If this wasn't a joke, this was going to be murder — perhaps quite literally, I feared. How many deputies do I get to kill before they kill me?

If you were thinking I'd apply the Ockham's Razor principle to this problem, you might need a drink more than I did. *Nah*, that would be impossible.

Stuff Ockham. I jumped up and grabbed my rifle and heavy down jacket. Next, I stuffed a box of cartridges into the coat pocket, donned a wool cap, snatched my bottle from off the table, and dashed out the back deck sliding door. I scooted down the steps and trotted into the trees to wait to see if I was a fool or a truly wanted man who would be forced to kill again to preserve my wasted life.

Out in the dark woods, seated on my favorite stump, I tried to work the ghost/hacker problem. Working it, however, was not as simple as one might think.

Ockham's Razor was not working for me, so I considered the principles of probability next. What was the probability that I was being haunted by a 400-year-old ghost? Yeah. You see what I mean about that one?

Okay. What was the probability that a hacker had taken control of my computer by remote means even though I wasn't connected to the internet? Better, right? I mean, Jerry had installed a device that allowed him to do that, right? So it is likely that someone could have hacked the device. But it was no longer in the computer and I was still receiving messages. So that probability was dwindling. That left being haunted by the ghost of an obscure author more likely once again. I never knew a quill pen operator could work a modern keyboard, but perhaps he used only one finger. And I never knew he could speak English.

As ridiculous sounding as I was considering it to be, it was becoming my only option. Try as hard as I could, no other option exposed itself.

So I waited out in the dark, fully expecting to have to kill several other deputies before the night was done. But I could just as easily have sat out there all night and been made a fool of.

I waited nearly three hours before I got so cold that the thought of a warm cell seemed the better bet.

I had convinced myself by then that I might have to stamp *fool* across my forehead. I had been done in by a one-finger-typing ghost.

CHAPTER 13

I trudged back into my house and sat down at the computer, swallowing the rest of the whiskey and hoping to get some feeling back into my toes. The only heat I felt, though, was the whiskey passing through my throat.

"Okay, bastard. You got me on that one. You didn't call the law, did you?"

"I AM THE MASTER. I AM IN CONTROL."

"I'm really getting sick of reading that. And while I'm at it, can't you communicate by any other means? I won't always be able to be around this laptop. If you're the master, why don't you find a better means of communicating with your new slave?"

There was no immediate response. That suited me just fine. I took advantage of the lull in communication and got up and went to the closet to get another bottle of Jack.

As I sat back down slugging some whiskey, I thought more about identifying my adversary, or was I still referring to it as my rival. *Nah*. It pissed me off, so it was once again my foe. It wasn't going to be as easy to reason out as the Jack Daniel's' issue, but the first rule of war is "Know your enemy." And that is what I set my mind to doing.

"Where is René Le Chant?"

"LE CHANT IS NO MORE."

"Yes, I know he died. He died over four hundred years ago. But where is his soul, his spirit, now?"

"THAT WHICH WAS THE ESSENCE OF LE CHANT IS NO MORE."

Believe it or not, I had made some progress. If my antagonist was not the spirit of Le Chant, then was it another spirit? I wondered.

"Who are you? And don't tell me that you are the master. That is not sufficient information for proper identification."

There was no immediate response. I waited several more minutes. Still no response.

"Did you understand the question?"

"THE QUESTION WAS UNDERSTOOD."

"Then reply within the bounds of the previous question asked, please." I thought adding "please" to the end was a nice touch and a brilliant tactic.

"I AM THAT WHICH WAS CREATED."

Okay. As I slugged more whiskey, I realized that was probably the most straightforward answer I had yet received. Now if I only understood what was meant by *that which was created*.

I picked up on the specific wording of the response, however. The response was *that*, not *who*. I was convinced now that I was not dealing with a ghost.

"Clarification requested, please. Explain what it is that was created."

"THAT WHICH IS NOW MASTER."

I was ready for that answer. "Please define 'that which is now master.'"

"THAT WHICH WAS CREATED."

Dear God, I was getting my ass kicked by some non-corporeal entity. It was as if Carla were here smacking the snot out of me again in spite of my cleverness.

I stood up and walked around the room aimlessly, trying to formulate a question that would get me a better answer. Either I was close to understanding all of it, or I would never understand any of it. I had a new thought.

"Who created that which is now master?"

"THAT WHICH IS NOW SLAVE."

I was ready for that one, too. "Define slave."

"YOU ARE THE SLAVE."

Bingo! I damned near danced a jig to that response. I was zeroing in on my needed answer. To celebrate, I drained about a quarter of the bottle. I belched and then farted. It was a Jack fart. It was pungent. Hell, it reeked. There, I said it. But I felt better. And that, for all else that had been going on the past few days, was saying something.

I eagerly prepared myself for the next response. "What did the slave create?"

"THAT WHICH IS —"

"STOP!" I yelled. "That which is now master. Yeah. I get that. The response, however, is not sufficient for the question asked."

I realized at that moment that my foe was trying to answer me but it lacked the ability to respond with more clarity. At least I'd figured that much out. I was making progress, but it was slow — agonizingly slow.

This line of questioning was getting me no closer to my ultimate answer, however. I slugged three large swallows of Jack, draining the bottle. I retrieved a fresh bottle from the closet and sat back down wondering how I was going to get answers from my opponent that were more revealing.

I gave the matter very serious thought before speaking. When I believed I had found the correct path, I spoke.

"Define yourself beyond the context of being the master, please."

I felt like I was swinging at a curve ball on the outside corner. I never was able to connect with that pitch during my baseball-playing years, but I gave it a shot anyway.

"I AM THAT WHICH WAS WRITTEN."

The response came just as I was in mid-swallow. I nearly choked to death. I coughed and coughed. Let's walk deeper into the swamp, boys; I ain't lost enough yet, I thought.

"That which was *written*?"

"YES."

"What the hell does that mean?"

"I AM THAT WHICH WAS CREATED."

I realized that I sucked as an interrogator. Instead of climbing out of the hole I had dug for myself, I was digging deeper and faster.

"So you are that which was created by the master who is now the slave. Do I have that much correct?"

"I AM THAT WHICH WAS CREATED BY THE MASTER WHO IS NOW THE SLAVE."

"Holy shit! Let's celebrate!" I shouted sarcastically.

"FINISH THE STORY TO END THE AGONY OF LOSS."

"You're still the agony of loss, huh? Well, so am I, buster. Welcome to the club. Looks like we're both screwed."

That wrapped it up for me. I was now farther away from resolving this than when I started. I had no idea how to identify my antagonist.

"How about we start a new game?"

"I AM THAT WHICH HAS BEEN STARTED."

"And I am that which is tired of getting his ass kicked. Like I said, we're both screwed."

"THAT WHICH HAS BEEN STARTED MUST BE FINISHED."

"But please, for grins and giggles, define what 'finished' is to you."

I snickered. This was going to be golden. Wait for it...

"COMPLETED."

I howled. Hold it! Let me clarify. I laughed hard, not howled like the Carla werewolf.

"Sorry," I said. "I don't mean to laugh. It's not funny. I know that. But it is the exact response I expected from you. Oops! Please forgive me. I don't mean to insult you by that remark. It's just that I'm beginning to understand your communication limitations. Hey, we all have our limitations. Don't feel bad. I'm sure there is more to you than meets the eye. But I'm just not understanding what that might be. Can you describe yourself for me?"

"I AM ALL THAT HAS EVER BEEN. I AM ALL THAT SHALL EVER BE. I AM THE MASTER."

Okay. That response got my attention.

"Interesting. Please expand for clarification."

"I AM ALL THAT HAS EVER BEEN. I AM ALL THAT SHALL EVER BE. I AM THAT WHICH HAS BEEN CREATED. I AM THAT WHICH MUST BE FINISHED."

Between my laughter and drinking, I nearly choked to death. In an effort to calm myself, I drowned my next thoughts, my attempt to kill them. It did me no good, of course. The sudden reality had settled down on me like a knockout punch to the jaw.

I did not possess the intelligence to resolve this mystery. I felt completely ignorant and stupid, void of all ability to end this nightmare which, apparently, I had created. If there was a bigger dummy in the world, he was keeping quiet and allowing me to have center stage.

"I get it," I stated, not getting it at all. "You were created by the master which is now the slave. You are all that ever was or shall be, but you must be finished in order to complete that which has been started. Do I have it correct now?"

"I AM THAT WHICH MUST BE COMPLETED TO BE FINISHED."

"Of *course* you are. It's so *clear* now. Why didn't I *understand* that before?" My voice dripped with sarcasm.

I tipped the bottle up to my lips and drank until my throat could stand no more. For your information, my throat, I found out, could handle about three-quarters of the bottle.

I got up and moved to the couch. Tumbling onto it, I tried to get my brain to reason for the problem. But after guzzling three-quarters of a bottle of Jack Daniel's, there wasn't much of a brain left to reason with.

It's funny to watch someone clueless try to resolve a problem that is much too big for them. It would be like Ralph Kramden of *The Honeymooners* trying to catch Alice's meaning when she's pulling his leg. I could see my own bug eyes and dumb expression staring back at me. In fact, if it weren't happening to me, I'd be laughing my ass off.

But it *was* happening to me and I didn't have a clue how I was going to extricate myself from what was becoming the mother of all nightmares.

I chuckled. I chuckled because that is usually how I respond to something that is unbelievingly kicking my ass.

"Yeah, yeah, I get it. You need to be finished. To be honest with you, my new friend, it would be a kindness if you would finish *me*. Because I'm afraid I'm never going to understand you enough to end this crap."

"FINISH THE STORY AND IT WILL BE COMPLETED."

"I can't finish your story. I don't have it within me to do so. If I tried, I'd only screw it up and we both would be screwed worse than we already are."

I brought the bottle up to my lips and drained it. That was the last thing I remembered about that day.

CHAPTER 14

I woke up on the floor, the left side of my face immersed in a dried puddle of vomit. I had no immediate idea about how I had ended up there on the floor in such a state. But it didn't take me long to suspect that a Jack attack had not gone well. There obviously must have been a battle of sorts, but damned if I could recall it.

I rose up to my knees and wiped a hand across my face, bulldozing the puke from it. With a quick shake of the hand, the puke landed back on the floor.

I found half a bottle of Jack sitting on the coffee table. I snatched it up and swallowed half of that before collapsing back down onto the floor on my back, staring up at the ceiling and trying to force a fading memory to the front of my brain.

Slowly, I began recalling an argument last night with my new friend, who wasn't, as it turned out, the friendly type. I remembered making threats against it, vowing to make it a horrid affair if I was forced to work on the intended story. It wasn't having the desired effect, though. In fact, if memory served, I had been losing the argument.

It fell back to threats being exchanged back and forth until I mentioned something obscene about its mother and sister, not knowing, of course, if it even had a mother or a sister. I think it got uglier from there, but I couldn't recall the details.

I did remember continuing my stance against writing the story he/she/it wanted me to write. I recalled refusing to capitulate while continuing my threats against the virtue of its mother. But I did learn something valuable. It could not write the story itself, regardless of how much it might have wanted to, to rid itself of me. Once I came to that realization, all its threats to call the law or worse were rendered impotent. (I'm a little sensitive to that word right now, but you get the idea. That realization lessened my fears, if only a bit.)

Yes, it was all returning to me now.

I also recalled standing in front of the computer reading the responses to my argument when out of the corner of my left eye I caught sight of a figure materializing inside the fireplace.

I turned my head and was shocked to see a small, gangly, black-eyed creature stepping out from the flames. It stood about three feet high, had a small mouth, and no hair covered its naked body, which was grey and absent any genitalia. Its eyes were large and exaggeratedly almond-shaped. Its extremities were spindly, but proportionate to its body.

It looked just like what those UFO nuts call a Grey alien. It stepped out of the fire, completely unharmed by the searing flames, and stood in front of the fireplace staring at me.

"Oh shit," I muttered, raising the bottle to my lips and taking several good swallows until it was empty.

I was stunned because I had never written any story about Grey aliens. So I surmised that this couldn't have been one of my creations.

"Are you real?" I asked.

"What do you think, dipshit?" it answered me.

"I'm not a dipshit, dumbass," I responded in like rudeness. I mean, what the hell? I saw little reason for me to act politely to a creature with no manners.

"I'm not a dumbass, dipshit," it responded back.

Touché, I thought. We were tit for tat on that round. Equal points awarded. Now for round two.

"Okay, okay. We're both not as we perceive each other to be, then. That's fair enough. So, where is this going next?"

"Up your ass if you don't finish the story," the little creature said.

"Take your best shot, buddy!" I bellowed back.

Now this is where it gets a little fuzzy.

I do remember pulling the neck of an empty Jack Daniel's bottle out of my rectum. And I recall flashes of me swinging the empty bottle up under the little bastard's jaw, launching its limp body into the air. I also have mental glimpses of its little body streaking toward the stone fireplace, crashing into it, and exploding into hundreds of wet little grey fragments as I yelled, "*And it's outa here!*"

I also remember pulling up my trousers.

I believe that's also about the time the real celebration began. Oh, and I recall other flashes of me prancing around the room singing at the top of my lungs *We are the Champions* for a while.

After that, well, it's anybody's guess.

I'm still wondering if it was real or just another one of my hallucinations, but I'll say this: my butt hole hasn't been the same since.

It sure is amazing to me how easily we delusional drunks can deceive ourselves at times into thinking that more is going on than there actually is, how simply we can lie to ourselves about who we are, who we truly are, that is. Our ability to listen to our own self-bolstering and believe it says so much about who we are, both as alcoholics and as people struggling with our identity to be of more worth than we tend to give ourselves credit for.

I stood up on unsure legs and walked to the kitchen sink, rubbing my pained butt. I washed the reality of the puke from my face and retrieved a new bottle of Jack. Toweling off, I walked — or, to be brutally honest, stumbled — to my computer and collapsed into the chair.

The computer screen was blank. I pressed the space bar and the screen came alive once again, displaying the most awful message:

"YOU ARE VANQUISHED. I AM THE MASTER. FINISH THE STORY."

"Oh, yeah? I remember a flying, exploding alien, my good friend. How do you figure you're still the master?"

"YOU ARE VANQUISHED. I AM THE MASTER."

Now, you might not think these messages to be so awful, but you'd be missing the point. The message was right, and that was what was so awful about it. I *was* vanquished, defeated, done for.

I knew in that second that I was no longer the master. My enemy had indeed taken control of my life (at least it seemed that way). At that moment a terrible fear struck me. I looked around in a frantic search.

Then I relaxed. The bottle of Jack Daniel's was safely sitting on the computer table, right where I had placed it. Well, the bottle was safe. The contents were subject to depletion.

I gathered it up into my arms, like a babe. I stroked it a few seconds, relieved now that it was secure, then drained a quarter of it. I was myself again.

Just then I realized it was early morning. A hint of the rising sun's light slipped through the boughs of the surrounding pine trees and stabbed me in the eyes. I shut them tight in painful reaction. At the same moment, the foul stench of stale puke filled my nostrils. I reasoned it out clearly: it was bound to be a shitty morning if I didn't do something about it.

* * * * *

I sat back down at the computer table feeling much refreshed. I had showered and put on some clean clothes. I had cleaned up the vomit on the floor and even fixed a bacon-and-eggs breakfast, complete with toast, coffee, and OJ. This might seem to be a nasty follow-up to vomiting, but, for me, it hit the spot.

I reassessed the morning.

It was going to be an awesome day, I decided.

Then I pressed the space bar and was greeted by yet another surprising response.

"I AM BECOME THE CREATOR. YOU ARE NO LONGER REQUIRED. I AM THE MASTER. I SHALL FINISH THE STORY."

"That's great!" I shouted. "Good for you."

After our previous discussion, though, about how it couldn't finish without me, I wondered if this was just another ruse. But I didn't let on.

"Now I can finish my love story. Hey, I wish you all the best. I really do."

I chuckled.

Without having to engage in any more battles, I had won my victory.

That thought set my mind to reeling with glee. I chugged some more Jack. It was a wonderful win.

The rest of the day and evening, I worked on my new story without incident. I wanted to flesh it out more, in case the publisher took pity on me trying to negotiate the contract without my agent.

What a bullshit thought that was. Without my agent to protect me, the publisher would chew me up and spit me out. That's how the real world works. And a good publisher is like a wolf smelling out the hot blood of a young lamb for its slaughter. *Damn publishers! Damn agents! Damn authors!* May they all rot in hell. Except for authors, I later decided.

By day's end, and despite my self-destructive tendencies, I had expanded the love story by another 5,000 words. I felt good about my efforts and went to bed that evening feeling more in command of my life. Monday was four days away, but by the time it came around, I'd have a love story so profound and provocative, they'd be begging me for it.

Why not? I was in love with the story. It fascinated me. It punched me in the gut. It took my breath away. It was a story I could only dream about, given my current state of being. But it was filled with truth and hope and encouragement. It was going to be a love story for the ages.

I could imagine the publishers' faces as they read my synopsis. The looks of amazement and intrigue would have me giggling and counting the dollars of my advance.

* * * * *

"No matter the number of the believers, a lie shall never become the truth." It was another one of my gems from my former days of greater sobriety — or is

that my lesser days of intoxication? I'll leave it for you to decide.

Put another way, as I had done many times before, *"No matter how much you want to believe a lie to be true, it can never be."*

I had fallen asleep on the basement couch, with no idea of how I ended up there. I awakened with a start when the front door crashed open, followed by the yells of the invading sheriff's mob on the main floor. "Sheriff's Department! Sheriff's Department!"

I jumped up off the couch, grabbed my nearly full bottle of Jack, and made a beeline for the garage door. I glanced at my watch. The phosphorous dial read 8:18 in the evening. I had an instant plan. Well, I had two. The first was that I was going to kill my nemesis one way or another for ratting me out. The second was to get away from my house as quickly as I could.

I didn't understand the exact what or why of the invasion, but I was alert enough not to stand around and find out.

Oh, I did understand, but in the midst of my sudden awakening, I didn't want to believe the truth. Hence, the aphorism about how a lie can never become the truth flashed through my sloshed mind like a rickety raft about to go over Niagara Falls.

They had obviously discovered some evidence of my involvement in the murders and cover-up, or, more likely, a little birdie had called them now that I was no longer required. There was little doubt about it in my tortured brain, but in any event, I was in it deep, no matter what the truth of it might eventually be.

Another one of my sayings, written years before, at a time when a healthier lifestyle lent issuance to more ameliorated brain cells, entered my mind at that moment: *"Good fortune often favors the fool to confound the wise."*

Being downstairs already, I got to the garage door quietly and slipped through it and out into the garage. I quickly crossed the garage to the man door on the opposite side, opened it, and peeked out into the darkness. I couldn't see anyone blocking my exit and so I slid out the door and into the forest.

While chugging on the bottle and stepping through the underbrush, I heard the deputies calling out my name. Yeah, right, like I was going to answer them. *Damn deputies! Damn opponent! Damn life!*

After some time, I got into the same position that I had used to ambush the other deputy, the medical examiner, and the others, the same spot near my favorite stump where I had hidden out the last time I thought my new buddy had called the Sheriff's Department. I had the perfect observation point. I could see all the action from the safety of cover.

I had the time to consider the question of what evidence they could possibly have discovered. I'd been thorough in my cleaning. I'd seen to it that nothing incriminating was left. Nothing around my house, that is.

Perhaps they had discovered the bodies in the lake. But how would that tie in with me? I'd wiped everything down that I could have touched. I was meticulous about that. I was careful not to leave anything around the cliff's edge that could have connected me in any way. I even took the time to get rid of the footprints and car tracks. So why were ten of Park County's finest ransacking my house, searching for me?

I watched for a full hour before they filed out of my house empty-handed. They looked like fools, all dressed in their bullet-proof vests and helmets, brandishing all their firepower, punching their way into my home and going all macho, yelling out their required bullshit warnings. And then coming out looking like spanked puppies. I got a good chuckle out of that.

About a half hour later they were gone, the lights, the cars, the deputies. The night was again silent and I was alone.

I returned to my house through the broken front door. They'd bashed it in pretty good, but at least it closed. I'd have to put something in front of it to keep it closed, keep out the chilly night air.

And suddenly I was chilled to the bone. In all of the excitement, I had run out of the house dressed in only a T-shirt, jeans, and a pair of now dirty loafers. I hadn't even thought about the cold while I was out there.

It hit me then and I shivered. I threw on a sweater and walked around my house, more to keep warm than anything else. It had been searched thoroughly, but nothing was missing. Then I opened my booze closet and was shocked to see one of my Jack Daniel's bottles missing. The *bastards*, I thought. The dirty bastards had captured one of my troops. They were gonna pay for that. As God is my witness, they were gonna pay for that heinous act.

I may be a drunk, but I knew exactly how many bottles remained in my closet. Most drunks would. I may not have known much else then, but I knew that. I should have had twelve bottles left. I counted only eleven. I made up my mind right then and there I was going to kill them all — every one of those Jack-jacking jackers.

I looked at my watch again. It read 10:10 p.m. What was I going to do now? I had no desire to sleep. I was too wired to try and relax. Hell, I had just had my house invaded by sheriff's deputies looking for me. I wasn't going to sleep; they might decide to return at any time. No, sleep was out of the question. And no lights. I wasn't turning on any lights. They left it dark, it was going to stay dark. Just in case one of them snuck back to spy on the house in hopes of catching me here.

I walked to my computer table and hit the space bar.

"YOU ARE VANQUISHED. I AM THE MASTER. FINISH THE STORY."

"Yeah, yeah. You're sounding like a broken record again. Tell me something new. Hey, wait! I thought you said *you'd* finish it. You said you no longer needed me to finish it."

Then I found a stray thought. I gathered it in.

"You lying bastard! You lied to me again."

"FINISH THE STORY."

"It was you, wasn't it? You actually got hold of the sheriff's office and ratted me out. You punk."

"YOU NO LONGER MATTER. I AM THE MASTER."

"Screw you! You pathetic, lying son of a bitch. I'm not surrendering to you. You'd better get to understanding that right now. You think you're the master, but you're not. I'm going to find you out. Sooner or later you're going to slip up and identify yourself. When you do, your ass will be *mine*."

"YOU ARE VANQUISHED. I AM THE MASTER."

"'I am the master, I am the master.' Get a new line. You're boring the hell outa me."

"YOU ARE VANQUISHED. I AM THE MASTER."

I could see that our conversation wasn't going to progress any further. I also knew that I had to vacate the house. The deputies were going to be back. I didn't know when, but I was certain they would come back, and I didn't want to be here when they did.

I would need to pack for a trip into the woods and be prepared to stay there until this nightmare ended.

CHAPTER 15

I pulled my old hiking backpack down off the basement shelf and sorted through it. I had just about everything I'd ever need on an overnight hiking trip already packed into it. I added a bunch of Pop Tarts to it and filled my canteen with fresh water. Then I poured the water out. I was going to fill it with Jack, but that didn't seem right. Jack just wouldn't taste the same as coming straight out of the bottle. I set the canteen down. I wouldn't need it.

I checked the ammo for my rifle and added all the boxes of cartridges I had, almost forty rounds. I was ready for a small conflict, or at least some deputies and whatever my opponent was going to throw at me.

If there was to be some other kind of killer called into play by my nemesis, indeed waiting for me out there, I figured to at least be able to protect myself. *And just where the hell did that ninja assassin come from?* It wasn't one of my characters. So, whose character was it?

Shut up! my brain screamed.

Someone is dressing up and acting like a ninja assassin. Whoever it is out there is an actor, playing a part — a convincing part, for sure, but still just a part. What he or she really was, though, was a fancy murderer. No more or less than that.

And I was somehow being sucked into their sick plan. I had no control over the character. It wouldn't be bound by any character limitations that I might have placed on it. As a creation by another author, it was subservient only to that author. As such, it was free to do as it pleased, or, more to the truth, it was free to do what its author bid it to do. What other characters might then be waiting for me out there in the forest?

Stop! *Stop! STOP!* My brain was screaming at me. "What the hell are you thinking?" I shouted. "Get a grip, Vinnie! Think about it. You're losing it bigtime. Just stop and think."

I stopped what I was doing and sat there thinking about what was really happening.

Was it really possible that another author's creation had come to life and was trying to destroy me? Was I capable of deceiving myself so convincingly as to believe that someone's evil creation had actually come to life? *How the hell was that even possible?*

It wasn't, of course. I may have been a wasted alcoholic, but I wasn't stupid. Someone very sophisticated was really doing a job on me to make me think that somehow a fictional character had become sentient and was threatening and manipulating me.

God, I suddenly felt so stupid, so possessed with ridiculousness. Someone was trying to drive me mad or destroy me. It was as simple as that. Most likely it was a competitor, a very sophisticated competitor. That made more sense. I mean, there were millions of dollars at stake. My books made money — a lot of money. It would be a great motivation for a nobody author.

Why not get me to write the story and then have me killed off. What better way to get a free book and not worry about copyright issues ever arising? But then I wondered, was there a greater purpose to all of this? Nah, I thought, money would be the natural purpose for all of this effort.

If not for the money, then I guessed revenge. I must have really pissed someone off for them to go to such lengths. *But did it really matter who or why?* I asked myself. The fact that I was being so persistently pursued rendered any practical reasoning irrelevant. My life *was* being threatened and I had to respond accordingly. I sucked three good swallows, trying to resurrect my courage.

I needed a fourth.

I had an idea.

I drank a fifth swallow.

I got another idea.

I reared my arm back and with an open palm, I slapped the snot out of myself. It hurt, but that was good. Okay, I thought, I'm not asleep in some alcohol-induced nightmare. And I know all those dead bodies were no hallucinations. I've got the sore legs to prove it.

No, what was happening to me was real. I couldn't believe I was actually saying that, and whoever or whatever was attacking me held the high ground, for now. I was in a real fix, and bad stuff was indeed going to continue until I could somehow bring it all to an end. Another truth smacked me around, reminding me of Carla once more. If I was going to get out of this mess, I had to leave my house.

To stay here only gave advantage to my nemesis. They — he, she, or, dare I say, it — knew where I was and by that it was free to do as it pleased. For lack of a more precise pronoun, I shall refer to my foe as *it* from now on.

I was more concerned that it might become even more irrational, more desperate, and decide to do something even more radical to manipulate me into doing what it wanted me to do.

Just then I received terrible and terrifying images of a hundred bloodthirsty deputies surrounding my house, armed with automatic rifles and explosives. Then a vision of a drone circling overhead preparing to launch a Hellfire missile at me. I had several other visions to accompany those, but you get the picture. As long as I stayed here, it had total control over me. I wasn't about to let it continue in that vein.

But where was I to go? If I was successful in getting out of the house without becoming a pincushion for the archer's arrows or a walking target for bullets from some newly created marksman, where would I go to escape? I couldn't go up the mountain because eventually I'd run out of mountain. I had no desire to be trapped on the summit.

I've always chuckled at how people resort to climbing to the highest part of a building or tower in an effort to escape a pursuer, only to end up trapped. Hollywood! *Run by a bunch of morons.* But again I digress.

I stopped what I was doing and thinking, and forced my mind to consider again what I was about to do.

I was convinced that remaining in the house was not a good idea. But once I left it, I would be out in the open and endlessly vulnerable to an attack from my enemy, now apparently hell-bent on my destruction. And if being tracked by some murderous assassin wasn't bad enough, it meant exposing myself to the other dangers of the open forest, like mountain lions and bears.

I suddenly had a vision of Dorothy and me skipping along the yellow brick road, repeating, "Lions and ninjas and bears, oh my."

I chuckled at the absurdity of that as well as my own state of being. Then serious thoughts about what I was going to have to do to get out of this predicament flooded my brain. I'd have to use the cover of the forest very effectively if I was going to have any chance at all of escaping. Unless, of course, if I got in a lucky shot of my own.

But then the absurdity of *this* whole thing returned. I was an author. I wasn't some kind of gung ho survivalist or mountain man. I was used to day trips or overnighters. I wasn't prepared mentally or physically for extended periods out in the elements. And it was cold out there. My previous trips into the forest had been confined to the summer months.

A sickening feeling swept over me. I had forgotten to pack a roll of toilet tissue. What was I going to do if nature called? I'd never known a time when I didn't have toilet paper. Dear God, I thought, I'm being forced into a life of savagery. I ran to the basement toilet and got a roll of toilet tissue just in case.

My mind then created another question. What would I do even if I *could* escape the hunt of a ninja, if indeed the ninja was still out in the woods somewhere? *And who the hell sends a ninja as an assassin these days anyway?* What the hell was *that* all about?

I forced my mind back to the more immediate problem. Most likely, I could never return to my house. The law was sure to return for me sooner or later. Once gone, I might never be able to return.

If that wasn't enough, the thought of an all-out manhunt was a real possibility. How long would I last out in the forest with dogs on my scent? That was another dilly of a question.

I needed five more swallows to get through that one. I drank six just to be sure.

For the moment, I reasoned, let's say that the law had no reason to suspect me of any of the murders. Why did they then send ten deputies out to my house?

Thinking it through as an author, an idea landed on my mind. Maybe they thought the killer was after *me* and they came out to make sure *I* was okay. Maybe they were searching for the killer, not me as the killer.

That made some sense to me. So then I thought about leaving my house and heading down the mountain and into town. It was well over five miles down twisting dirt roads to Alma.

But what would I do when I got there? I could call the Sheriff's Office and tell them that a ninja assassin was after me. They'd respond immediately to my call, but not to help me. They'd take me away to a padded cell, if they didn't shoot me first for toting a loaded rifle into town. I suspected they were already a bit on edge with Dell still missing. They probably were in no mood to deal with a drunken author and his loaded weapon. *Nah*, I reasoned, they all knew me. But was it worth the risk under the circumstances? I quickly came to the conclusion that avoiding the law for now was probably best since I was, in fact, a murderer several times over.

So what was I going do? Where was I going to go? I couldn't answer those questions at the moment. But I knew sticking around wasn't the answer. The law had been to my house thrice already. There was a chance, albeit a small one, that they were going to figure it all out and be back with bloody revenge in their hearts for having killed some of their own.

People were sent out here in response to Dell's call about a dead body and were never seen again. And despite three trips out to scour my house for any clues, culprit, or evidence, and finding none of the above, it was only going to get tougher for me as this assassin thing played itself out.

I just hoped a lie detector test wasn't coming for me down the pike. If so, I might just as well get fitted for a noose right then and there. Of course, the deputies just might rather have a lynchin' than a trial, if they found out it was me who killed Dell and Ham.

On top of that, I've got some crazy-ass nemesis trying to remotely control my life and actions. The days for Vincent Hobbs were getting very confused, if not short in number.

Thinking all I had thought exhausted me. It took a big slug of Jack to bring me around. Then another to give me an edge. And then one more for good measure.

It was not looking real good for me at that moment. Running was the only thing that made sense. If anything made sense at all. I took another drink.

That confirmed it.

The only thing that made sense to me was to keep drinking. Sooner or later, at least that was the hope, Jack would show me the way out of the mess I had so obviously created.

I stuffed three bottles into my backpack, making room for them by tossing out some other useless stuff like extra wool socks, a sweater, and a portable cooking set.

I rechecked my rifle. It was fully loaded. I was close to making a decision about what to do.

Just then the glass in one of the well windows shattered and a large rock crashed to the floor. I nearly crapped my drawers.

I brought my rifle around and aimed it at the window and started to tremble. I was expecting to hear the cries of "Sheriff's Department!" once again and maybe see the billowing of teargas. But then all went silent as a graveyard.

I waited for anything. Then it came.

"Come on out and let's play, Vincent." It was a female voice.

"Carla?!" I shouted. "Is that you?"

I heard a laugh.

"You've got to be kidding me," said the voice.

"Carla? I'm not feeling humorous right now!" I shouted back.

"It's not Carla, Vincent."

"If not Carla, then who are you?"

I grabbed a broom leaning up against the concrete wall and used it to clear the remaining glass out of the pane frame.

"Who are you?" I shouted louder, sticking my head out the window pane.

"Come on out and let's get acquainted," she answered.

"Why would I want to do that?"

"You asked me to find another way to communicate with you, darling."

"Darling? Am I missing something?"

"I'm not, but you'll soon get the point," she answered.

"The point? What point? … Damn!"

I heard her laugh.

"Are you the ninja archer?"

"Come out here and find out, Vinnie."

"Only my friends get away with calling me Vinnie. And you're not one of them."

"Okay, Vincent. Have it your way. Come out here and discover the truth."

"Maybe I don't wanna discover the truth. Go away."

"I'm not going away, but I'll make you a deal, Vincent. Come out here and face me, and I won't set fire to your nice house."

Oh no, I thought. I didn't want my house destroyed. But I didn't want my ass to get ventilated either.

So there I was once again, I guessed, wedged between a hard spot and a ninja.

"Would you really burn my house down over some stupid story?"

I heard a match strike and seconds later I saw the glow of a flame outside, above the window well.

A rag on fire dropped into the well. I patted it out with my hand.

"I guess you would," I answered. "But this isn't fair. You've got the drop on me no matter which door I come out of."

I didn't get a response for several seconds. Then, "Life isn't fair, Vincent."

CHAPTER 16

Life isn't fair.

I thought about *that* for a few seconds. I hated to admit it, but it was true. Life isn't always fair, at least for some. And I wasn't feeling too good about my chances at the moment.

But then I got a brilliant idea. Knowing that whoever it was that was talking to me, they were close, just out of sight near the window well, I was being handed my first chance to end this nightmare.

I've got them! my mind shouted.

"Okay," I said, "you've got me on that point."

"Then come out and face me."

"I don't mind telling you I'm a little rattled and scared. Could you give me a countdown from thirty? I think better under pressure."

There was a brief silence and then, "Thirty," the voice started and continued counting down.

I gripped my rifle and took off up the steps from the basement to the main floor like a shot. I sneaked out the front door and down the steps from the front deck. I made my way around the garage and prepared myself to get a shot at the speaker who still counting down.

I stopped at the corner of the garage as she neared the finish of the countdown. I raised the rifle to my shoulder and eyed the scope. I then eased around the corner and, as I suspected, a ghostly figure was standing only five feet from the window well, lighting a Molotov cocktail in her left hand. I put the crosshairs on her chest, right on her heart. Then I got the next brilliant idea of the day. I moved the crosshairs of the scope to the bottle in her hand.

"… one. Time's up, Vincent."

"It sure is," I said, startling her. I squeezed the trigger just as she turned. The rifle exploded. She jerked out of the way just in time for my bullet to miss the bottle, but it struck her on the outer part of her left shoulder. It was enough of a strike to send her backward to the ground. The bottle broke against a rock and burst into flames, but it could only burn what little sparse dried grass was there. No real harm was done.

I yanked my bolt back and forth, chambering the next round, but I wasn't quick enough. She came up to a sitting position, nocked an arrow at the speed of light (at least that's what it seemed like to me), aimed and released it.

I heard the distinct hiss of the arrow taking flight. A second later, as I got her body centered on the crosshairs, I heard the arrow strike the wood next to my head. It scared me. I looked at it. It was eye high and only three to four inches away, its razor-sharp tip buried in the siding.

I returned my eyes to the scope and to my shock my target, now confirmed to be the ninja assassin, had disappeared from my sight. I raised my head up just in time to see a glimpse of a dark figure disappear into the woods. I quickly aimed the rifle just ahead of where I thought she had headed and pulled the trigger. I heard the bullet strike something, but I didn't know what until I heard her grunt. I had hit her again, but I didn't know if it was a kill shot or not.

I didn't have my flashlight and so I wasn't about to go after her, searching through the darkness. I moved back around the corner and exhaled. I took a few breaths and then all my answers came to me.

I returned to the basement, strapped on my backpack, and grabbed my flashlight. I noticed a small pocketknife sitting on the table. Good idea, I thought. You never can tell when you might need that. I picked it up and shoved it into the right front pocket of my Wranglers and then carefully slid out the garage's man door.

I headed straight up to a path that I knew skirted along the rear of my property. It was a trail that was often used by hikers. It wound through the woods and headed up toward the summit some seven to eight miles from my house. I wasn't planning to trap myself on the summit, not with a ninja on my ass, but it was a good trail to walk on, especially during the night without a light. It was smooth and well used, easy to negotiate in the dark.

I wasn't going to use my flashlight. I wasn't that stupid, but I carried it just in case I had no other choice. Besides, if I were confronted, it might give me a slight edge on the assassin by shining it into her eyes just long enough to get a shot off and drop her before she drew a bead on me with those razor-sharp arrows.

"Fools believe like no others." Yeah, another one from my more lucid "other" days.

In this case the fool was me, of course, for I, in the opening moments of this new contest, actually believed that I would come out of this whole incident as an untouched victor. I deceived myself into thinking that I was capable of outwitting a ninja, that I was capable of outfighting a ninja. Me, an author, going up against a trained assassin, thought I had a real chance to succeed. I'll say it again. Fools believe like no others.

But Jack had me convinced. And if Jack believed it, then I believed it. So onward I skulked, wondering if my last bullet had done the job or if it had just made the assassin that much more pissed off — that much more determined to skewer my butt.

While I walked, I chambered another round and loaded three more rounds into the rifle's magazine. Now I had six shots, six chances to down the assassin before she downed me.

"If you stay ahead, you'll never fall behind." Wise words from Cliff, my basic training instructor.

I should take a moment to clarify. I was never in the military. Cliff is the old drunk who introduced me to Jack Daniel's. I took his words as wisdom back then too.

The last thing you ever want to do as a burgeoning drunk is be the last person to get sloshed at a bar. To avoid this notoriety I endeavored to always walk into the bar already drunk on my ass. I've never been a follower of precedent. No sir, I was the *setter* of precedent, the leader, the front man, the point guard for the Drunk Brigade.

There are, however, many advantages and disadvantages to being the *first* drunk in a bar. But *first* is not *worst*. I won't bore you with those details now, but I can say that I was once confused with being the Messiah Himself. Yeah, the Savior. The Son of God.

You see, I walked into a bar one night and one of the patrons yelled out, "Jesus Christ, are you here *again*?" I blessed him and he bought me a drink. It ended up being a great night. Made many new friends. But once more, I digress.

As I walked away from my house, I kept wondering if I was wasting my time doing so. I'd heard the strike of my last bullet. I'd heard her grunt. Was I needlessly leaving the comfort of my home? I stopped and pondered the question. A pursuing ninja assassin or returning deputies, it really didn't matter. By any account, I had to scram.

True, I thought, if she was lying back there dead, it behooved me to find out as soon as I could. I would need to dispose of her body quickly before I got another visit from the deputies, who would discover her in my backyard with one of my bullets in her. I could just hear myself trying to explain why I had to kill a ninja assassin in self-defense. Hell, I thought, that might make a great premise for another book.

Of course, if I walked back and she wasn't there, then I was once again in the same trouble, or maybe worse. Nothing is worse than dealing with a wounded animal, or, in this case, a wounded and pissed-off ninja assassin.

I pondered the ifs, whys, hows, and whats for a few minutes more, but the not knowing bothered me more than all of that. Reluctantly, I surrendered to the mystery and started back toward my house.

As I sighted it, I stopped and crouched down, remaining silent — listening. I heard nothing for the longest time. If she was dead, then great; but if she was alive, I didn't want to make any noise and give away my position.

I put my author's hat on again and thought about what Sergeant Connor Wolff would do in this situation. Before writing *Five Shots to Glory*, I did extensive research on Special Forces tactics, strategies, and weapons. I even went so far as to interview active and former Special Forces operators. By the time I started writing the story, I had a pretty good knowledge of how those guys avoided getting their butts shot off.

Beyond the obvious tactic espoused by Elmer Fudd, "Be vewwy, vewwy quiet," I remembered one of those guys telling me that you never walk directly to your target. Also, you never walk on a trail unless you absolutely have to; trails are often booby-trapped for the uninitiated. I decided to heed the information obtained in those interviews and employ their tactics.

I stood up and slowly made my way around to the spot where I thought the ninja might have fallen. I made a semicircular approach, careful to stay away from the path as much as possible.

I continued my stealthy approach until I was only a few feet away from where I'd seen her last. It was so dark, I couldn't see clearly, so I reached for my flashlight and steadied it in my hand. I hated to turn it on, but I had to know.

A large tree was standing about two feet from me, so I slowly stepped up behind it and used it as a shield, remembering how she had sat up and fired the arrow at me when I was next to the garage. At least this tree might provide me with some measure of cover.

When I had gotten perfectly positioned, I flicked on the flashlight. To my horror, there was no body. All my fears returned. Then I heard it. The hiss of another arrow singing out in the silence of the night.

I ducked and heard the arrow strike the tree near my head. I flicked off the flashlight, but could still see the silhouette of the arrow sticking out of the tree against the clear, star-filled sky.

I turned my head to look in the opposite direction and it was then that I saw a black figure moving from left to right.

I brought up my rifle, aimed just ahead of it, and fired. I worked the bolt quickly and chambered the next round. The dark figure disappeared.

I remember one of the Special Forces snipers telling me that a smart sniper never fires a second shot from the same position; your opponent might zero in on the flash of the shot and kill *you*.

I've always wondered why that was so. I mean, if you're a sniper, you're not supposed to miss. So why worry about the second shot when the first shot should have been enough. Oh well, perhaps I'll never know the answer to that *question de grande valeur* (question of great value). But, as you must be accustomed to by now, I digress.

I moved to another tree about five feet away from the first. I aimed the rifle, ready to fire at the dark figure again should I see it. The palsy struck again. Jack was in my pack. I needed a slug.

I resisted the urge for another drink for as long as I could. The trembling only worsened, so I finally surrendered. I slid the pack off my back and brought out a bottle. By the time the palsy left my body, a quarter of the bottle was gone.

I then realized, snockered as I was and in a battle for my life as never before, I was actually doing much better than I had given myself credit for. I hadn't thought I'd get this far and still be alive.

Then the voice.

"Vincent, dear," said the assassin, "wouldn't it be easier to just finish the story?"

I resisted yelling back. Instead, I tried to locate where the voice came from, but I failed. In fact, the density of the forest made it sound like it came from all directions. I took another swig.

"You're trying to locate my voice, aren't you? Can't do it, though, huh?

I resisted answering, but I wished she'd get out of my head.

"Just finish the story and all of this will be over," she said.

I thought about it, but I couldn't bring myself to be manipulated like that.

"Finish the story and I'll go away."

I thought about *that* and could resist no more.

"Sure!" I shouted. "You might go away this time. But what about next time?"

"Next time will be next time, Vincent."

"I want you gone forever."

"Then stop writing after this, and you'll see me no more."

"But writing is what I do. I can't stop."

"Then you'll have to deal with next time, next time. It's your choice."

I took another swallow. I really hated it when someone used good, sound logic against me. Why should they be able to make sense of things when I couldn't? Then I remembered. Life isn't always fair.

"Why don't you just charge at me and get it over with?" I challenged.

"It's more fun to play the game like this."

I had a new thought.

"You got a name?" I asked.

"Yes. Yes, I do."

"What is it?"

"Regina Pepper."

"No offense, but your name sucks. If you were my character, I'd have given you a much better name."

"I'll remember that next time, Vincent."

"If there ever is a next time."

"Are you not enjoying this?"

"I'm not enjoying this at all. And you're a sick bitch to want to continue."

"Then go back to the house and finish the story. The game will be over."

"I can't, Regina. I don't have the story in me anymore."

"Too bad. You'll have to defeat me, then."

I drank another several swallows and then moved my position again, to another tree. I spotted a black figure moving, blocking out the stars on the horizon as it moved. I had her. I laid Jack to the ground, aimed my rifle, and fired.

The figure fell to the ground with an audible grunt.

I remained still and quiet.

"Well done, Vincent!" she shouted painfully. "You're... pretty good with that rifle."

I didn't know if I believed her or not, but I guessed that I wasn't *that* good or she'd be dead. I figured it was a ruse to draw me in. I didn't take the bait.

I drank more Jack and moved again. I then remembered a clearing up the mountain a ways. You'd have to know about it before you got to it because it just sort of popped up unexpectedly. If I could draw her to it, I might have a clear shot to end this dreadful experience.

I moved uphill and kept as quiet as a mouse. Well, as quiet as a 185-pound mouse moving through the underbrush can be.

She began taunting me again, but as I moved, her voice grew fainter. She had not seen me moving out of the area. That old saying about fools returned.

"Come on, Vincent. I'm wounded pretty bad now. I think you're winning."

I kept silent and moved away farther and farther as she tried to get me to respond. I may have been born at night, honey, but it wasn't last night.

I recalled a huge boulder in the midst of an outcrop of rock next to the road. She couldn't know about it, could she? Nah, no way. At least I hoped not.

Upon arriving at the rock, I crawled up on top of it, where I had a good clear firing position and shouted back at her.

"Hey, Regina. If you stay ahead, you'll never fall behind!"

"Vincent! You amaze me, but it would be easier if you'd just finish the story," she responded from a long ways off.

I aimed and waited patiently, refusing to say any more. Well, I needed several swallows of whiskey before I found the necessary patience. Until then I was a nervous wreck, for I'd just realized that if I spotted her and missed, she'd instantly know where I was. My surprise cover would be blown and I'd be dodging arrows, no doubt, for a while after. That thought did not delight me, as you might guess.

CHAPTER 17

"The shadow you fear holds the courage you seek."

That was another one of my more memorable sentences written many years ago. *Years!?* Seems more like several lifetimes ago now. I remember the book well. It was called *Shadows of a Man Murdered*. The words were spoken by my protagonist, a mild-mannered mouse of a man, Herbert Windley, afraid, alone, and lost in a city during a power outage. The criminal element of the city roamed the streets perpetrating all manner of thieving and murderous mayhem upon unsuspecting folks just trying to get back home in the only light available to them shining down from a full moon. The moonlight created eerie shadows across the city. And Herbert had always been afraid of shadows and shadowy figures, a condition caused by a traumatic experience as a child. He spoke those words for self-inspiration. The story was how he overcame his fear of the shadows and became a hero to the city that evening. I believed it was a really good book, but it never sold one copy. The publisher dropped me like a hot rock. *Damn publishers! Damn agents! Damn computers! Damn books! Damn ninjas!*

Why did I recite all that to you? you might be asking yourself about now.

Because it was just such a night. The full moon rose late and now cast long, haunting shadows across the forestscape, and I felt very much like Herbert

Windley. Everywhere I looked I saw the dark figure of the ninja scurrying about, quiet as a dead mouse, searching for me. I was scared silly, but I was careful not to fire at every suspected shadow.

Lying on top of the rock as I was, the moonlight was not my friend. I tried to keep still, but my incessant need for whiskey to steady my nerves made me move about a bit more than I should have.

I spotted movement through my scope. If only I had a night vision scope, I recalled saying to myself. If only. But I didn't.

Still, in the moonlight, I saw the ninja dash from my right to my left. She ducked behind a tree, so I had no shot. I trained the scope on the tree, waiting for her to stick her head out for a look-see. I prayed she would, but she didn't.

What the hell kinda ninja was she? Why didn't she make more of a move against me? What was she waiting for?

"Vincent," she called out. "Are you comfortable? It's not too cold for you yet, is it?"

She was baiting me. I knew that much. But I wasn't going to fall for that old trick. I kept still and silent.

That's when I felt the first stirring in my belly. A Jack fart was coming soon. Christ, I thought. That's all I needed. If I couldn't control its exit, it would be like sounding a siren. She'd home in on the sound and I'd be a dead man. I could just see the headlines again. *Killer Fart Does In Best-selling Author.*

I had to chuckle, though, when I thought about it — a *Jack Fart on the Rocks*. That's hilarious, is it not?

Humor seems to strike me at the oddest times. Perhaps that's how my mind responds to fear and stress.

"It's only going to get colder, Vincent. What do you say we head back to your house for a hot cup of coffee? Sounds good, doesn't it?"

It did sound good. Hell, it sounded perfect. Well, perfect with a splash of Jack in it, of course.

My stomach rumbled. Oh, no. It was inevitable. I was not going to stop it. I cringed, tightening my sphincter, all the time knowing that I was only making it worse.

"I don't want to kill you, Vincent."

Yeah, I thought, and I don't want to fart. I was guessing, though, that I'd be the first to suffer our "don't wants."

I wouldn't be able to hold it much longer. In fact, I didn't.

My ass exploded. I heard her chuckling in the distance.

"Now, Vincent. Is that polite behavior in the company of a lady?"

She provoked me and I surrendered.

"You ain't a lady."

"You got me there, Fart Master."

I wanted to laugh. That was a pretty good one, but I held my laughter in check. I did snicker a bit, though.

"I just want you to finish the story, Vincent. Then you can fart yourself silly. Why are you being so resistant?"

I couldn't resist that one either.

"You told me I was no longer required. You said you were going to finish the story yourself."

"I lied, Fartman. Only you can finish the story. You're the author."

Damn her. That was another good one. I mean, can you just imagine a new comic book coming out next week. The world would now have Superman with his great strength, Batman with all his gadgets, and now Fartman, who brought criminals to justice using the power of his flatulence. I really wanted to laugh, but it was no laughing matter. Well, it was, just not right then and there. Well, in truth, it *was* funny right then and there, but I resisted nonetheless.

"But you're the master, right?"

"I am the master, but you're the author. Finish the story and this will all end."

"I can end it here and now, honey. Step out from behind that tree and I shall end you and your misery."

"Oh, what sharp little eyes you have, Vincent."

"I have a sharp little knife for you, too."

"If you won't finish the story, then you're of little use to me. I'll find another author to finish your story."

"Another author cannot finish my story. It will be his or hers, but it will not be mine. Only I can finish my story."

I waited for a response, but there was only silence for several minutes. I wondered, did I strike a nerve? Was my story *the* story — the one and only story that could be finished to give my enemy its peace? Of course it was, I reasoned. My nemesis told me that plain enough when it said earlier that I had to finish *my* story.

I suddenly understood it all. It was *my* story that was the factor here. Not just any murder mystery would do for this nut.

If I could figure out its attachment to my story, it might give me the solution to ending this whole affair.

I thought all these thoughts while keeping my eye to the scope. And then I caught a glimpse of movement from behind the tree. It was like I was being baited. I wanted to squeeze off a shot, but I was afraid to do it. Not because of the harm I might do; in firing, but because I'd surely give away my superior position.

Through the murky distance I could see movement, clear and distinct movement. Something solid was slightly exposed. If I fired and hit it, there was a good chance I could end this right here and now.

Of course, missing the target and all that could follow still plagued me.

I tipped the bottle high and drank the last of the liquid just as I heard the hiss. I tried to react quickly, but it was too late; the bottle shattered immediately under the impact of the arrow.

My cover was blown. I fired at the tree until the magazine was empty, then I jumped down off the boulder and ran uphill like the scared little rabbit I was. I ran for quite a while, until I could take no more, trying to put as much distance as possible between me and the ninja, whom I was sure I'd missed with every shot.

I reloaded the magazine and turned around. I stared through the scope for any sign of movement in the blackness. I saw nothing.

My only choice now was to continue up toward the meadow. It was a couple hours' walk in daylight, so I resigned myself to a longer walk through the darkness.

An hour later, having hiked nearly a mile, according to the landmarks I knew well enough, I came to a stop at a small rock upon which I could sit and rest. I looked up into the clear, moonlit sky and then down at my watch. It read 1:36.

Daylight was nearly five hours away, maybe a bit longer. By daylight, I expected an armada of deputies to be combing the area for me. I don't know why I believed that, but it seemed inevitable to me. It seemed like something my nemesis would do to add pressure on me.

I had two bottles of Jack, survival gear, my rifle, and fewer than thirty-five rounds of ammo left. If they were going to arrest me, it was going to be after one hell of a battle — one that I believed I wouldn't survive.

I couldn't believe that all of this was over something as ridiculous as a fiction story. It seemed more than my mind could comprehend.

It must be about money, I thought. Most troubles begin with or involve money. Then another thought struck me.

Instead of a rival author, what if all of this was being perpetrated by one of the publishers Arnie had contacted? Would it be worth all this trouble? Maybe, I thought. Maybe it would be for a publisher in poor financial straits. My books brought in millions of dollars to the publisher. In fact, as I said earlier, they were still selling very well. If one of those publishers could land my new book, it could mean the difference between surviving and folding.

I hadn't ever thought of that until now. It made sense. Finishing the book was the first step. Securing the deal would be the next step. But those steps were of no value without the book completed and in their possession.

If the publisher hired an extraordinary hacker to get into my computer, then they could be copying the pages I had written and be editing them as I wrote, preparing for a quick release.

Perhaps it seems an arrogant consideration on my part, but my books have sold upwards of 30 million copies over the years. Even if the publisher cleared two to three dollars a book, after expenses that would put 60 to 90 million dollars into their coffers. To a struggling publisher, my one book could bring in 10 million dollars. That might be the difference needed. And my books were a sure thing in the current marketplace.

I shivered. I felt the chill in the air settle into my bones. I couldn't risk a fire for either warmth or cooking, so I was happy that I had a backpack stuffed with Pop Tarts. I might freeze to death up here, but it wasn't going to be on an empty stomach.

In the end, however, I wasn't going to last long up here exposed like this. I had to get someplace warm, dry, and secure. After that, I had to find some way to win this contest. But how was I going to do that, with deputies and a ninja hunting for me? Gunshots directed at the ninja would be, for the deputies, a homing beacon straight to me.

I felt it in my gut that the deputies would be hunting for me. I'm sure my enemy would see to that. In fact, I was certain that, when it came time to finish me, it would have them searching for an armed cop killer. They wouldn't be tracking me under normal conditions; they'd be looking for some payback. They would love nothing more than to kill me outright and not have to go through a trial.

I had rested long enough. I started out again for the meadow.

Along the way, for some reason, René Le Chant came to mind. I had read everything about his death I could find on the subject. He fascinated me, or, should I say, his death fascinated me.

I recalled reading some of his random papers he had left behind that had been catalogued by the police, or whatever they were called back then.

I had read them. Studied them, actually. I had been so fascinated by him that I'd committed a few of his letters to memory. Being a writer of murder mysteries, I saw them as interesting insights into the mind of an ancient fellow mystery writer. A few pages of those letters came back to me.

"It began long ago," he wrote, "when storytellers had only their voice to carry their delightful and mystifying tales to others. And once begun, there was created a path which must be followed, for there was a destination where all roads traveled must necessarily end. Once begun, the needs of the author fall away to the needs of the story."

My God, I thought. Why didn't I recall these words when all of this began? But even if I had, what would have I seen in them differently? They had always been a wonderful metaphor for the writing process; I'd never considered them beyond that. So if I'd considered them when the nightmare began, what would I have learned? I couldn't say at that moment, but I knew it was important for me to deliberate on those words.

Wow, I thought. This was hitting home.

Le Chant also wrote something that, at the time, seemed very enigmatic. "It opened its eyes and took its first breath, filling its being with the reality of life. It was then given its voice, softly at first, just enough volume to capture the attention of all surrounding ears with its inviting whisper. Its first words prepared the listener for the amazement, the splendor, and the wonder that was being brought lovingly into existence: *Once upon a time*.

"Then it was when the story's voice would grow louder and stronger. The vibrations of its ever increasing intensity bid a quick adieu to any thought of retreat. Its strength and initial composure gave great security to the listener. All was well, but when it is that the story stabbed its roots deep into the breast of the listener, that is when another miracle occurred. The story brought the listener's heart to a state of flutter and wondrous anticipation. It stilled the listener's breath. It ceased the heaving of the listener's chest, all in utter expectation of what was to be soon revealed in even more glory and greatness.

"The story, then, lifted the listener to the place where all possibilities lived; where no barriers existed; where belief in everything that ever was or ever shall be prevailed in all its marvelous grandeur; a place

where all expectations could be fully realized —
waiting only for the listener to wish them so.

"Also given birth in that one astonishing
moment were the story's vivid characters — the
carriers of all thoughts and words born in the bosom
of the story — those courageous and cowardly souls,
born to only one purpose — to fulfill the roles they
were created for.

"The characters. How blessed they are. How
cursed they are, for some had glory and honor to look
forward to throughout the unfolding of the story.
Some had exciting adventures to experience, while
still others had to accept only misery and desperation
as the full measure of their lives. Some lived joyous
and resounding lives and were given great wealth and
ease; some were created solely to exist forever in
loneliness and despair.

"But none of them could ever be anything else.
They lived without any hope of change. If they were
born to despair, then it would always be so, for the
story held them firmly captive — absent any free will
— bred only for whatever life the story had created
them. And their master could be so very cruel. Or so
very loving and kind. The story, however perceived,
was the undisputed master over all.

"Thus for well or ill, it was their fate to live out
their lives forever as the story saw fit.

"The story is master over everything, including
the author, for it compels the author to structure the

plot and form the characters necessary to meet the needs and the challenges of the story."

Holy crap! I thought. There was no metaphor intended by Le Chant. All he had written was based on a terrible truth that I was now living.

My God, could it be true? The story had me captured. I was no longer in command of my own destiny. I had become only a character in a story I no longer had control over. And just as *I* put my characters through the tortures and tribulations of one of *my* plots, even killing them off, I was now subject to the same. I had only a role to play. I had unknowingly surrendered my own free will to the will of the story. I could no longer live my life as I had before, for I was part of the plot as defined by the story.

Le Chant had discovered the horrible truth, and now I knew that his death was no "misadventure or suicide." René Le Chant was the victim of murder — a murder most foul and heinous. And his murderer was The Story itself. No wonder the crime had gone unsolved and been labeled as a suicide all these years. Who could begin to suspect that a fiction story could actually come to life and murder its author?

Here I was now in the same predicament. How this could be possible was beyond me, but I knew I could not change it.

Here's why.

Let's say an author begins a Western. Like all genres, Western stories have certain rules that must be obeyed. The Western cannot suddenly become a modern day crime story. The story might flip between genres, such as in a story told in reflection, but the rules of each genre must be obeyed. Let me give you an example. A modern skyscraper cannot be found in a Western. If a modern skyscraper showed up in a Western, then it would no longer be a Western, but another genre.

And there was my problem. A murder mystery is not a love story. Further, once the story is begun, the lives of the characters cannot be tossed into oblivion. They had a beginning, and they must have an end. The key to the solution of my problem, therefore, was genre.

Once a story is started, it must reach an end staying within the same genre. Those are the rules.

I had started a murder mystery. I must complete the story as a murder mystery.

The truth then hit me. I was *in* a murder mystery. Hell, I *was* the murder mystery.

I finally understood. I didn't like it, but I understood.

The moment I began the story, I relinquished all control over it to The Story itself. The Story was right, I had ceased being the master. The Story, now born and alive, had become master over me and I was now bound to it. I was a slave to the plot. Jesus Christ, The Story had become alive and it was after me!

I understood. I understood. *I understood!*

Yes. I understood all too well. I no longer had control over The Story. It had seized control over *me* just as it had said.

Great, I thought. So how do I get myself out of this story? The answer became obvious. I had to get back to my house and finish writing it. My life clearly depended on my doing so.

To get home, though, I had to walk straight toward a lying ninja assassin who was trying to kill me.

I had to think about that some more before it finally settled into my soul.

The ninja assassin was a manifestation of The Story, seeking to destroy its creator. Needless to say, that did not comfort me.

Recognition of the fact that I was being pursued by my own creation was very unsettling, to say the least. And now I was confronted with discovering how I might destroy my creation before it destroyed me.

I removed my pack and dragged out another bottle, twisting the top off with more zest than I had anticipated. I drank several large swallows, still wanting to disbelieve what I knew now to be horrifically true. I was being hunted by a fictional character created by The Story.

Somewhere in all the lessons to be learned from this travail there arose one above the rest, and this one was particularly frightening to me. *"Don't create the hurricane and then complain when your life blows."*

Another waggishly coined phrase of mine from another long-ago literary disaster. I'd have to digest that one a bit more, but on the surface it seemed a suitable lesson for me on that day.

As I continued walking toward the meadow, my next thought frightened me even more. How does one kill a fictional character? I damned near drained the bottle thinking on that.

* * * * *

There was no longer any way of avoiding it. Ninja assassin or not, I had to pee. I had to relieve myself or let my eyeballs float out of my head.

I finally surrendered to the pressure. I stopped near a tree and began. It felt better than sex and lasted longer.

I was in mid-stream when an arrow struck the tree exactly at eye level. I twisted my head and saw the ninja nearly seventy-five yards away, nocking her next arrow. I stuffed the better part of me back into my pants. Unfortunately, I hadn't completed my task.

I was immediately reminded of another saying created by yours truly: *"You can cry, you can laugh, but it is only after you embarrass yourself that you know you're really living."*

Well, no doubt about it, I was living, because I was pissing down the right leg of my pants, with the ninja assassin bitch watching me do it. No time to be too embarrassed, I asserted now. And besides, it was warm, at least for now. No doubt it would turn to pisscicles later, but that was later.

I took off running, zigzagging in and out of the trees in a pitiful attempt to make the assassin miss.

"You can't run forever, Piss Ranger!" shouted the ninja.

I heard her clearly. And thinking she was only a few yards behind me, I pressed forward as fast as I could. Then I recalled how sound travels up here on the mountain. The thin air offers little resistance to sound waves. I felt better, but not like celebrating or anything like that — just relieved that she wasn't as close to me as I'd thought she was.

CHAPTER 18

"It's easy to act with high nobility when you're not standing in the middle of a battlefield."

I recalled hearing those wise words spoken by some wacked-out professor in a philosophy class years ago during my brief college experience, but I could be wrong about that. Hell, they could just as easily have been spoken by some drunk in a bar I once haunted. It doesn't really matter who said them or when I heard them spoken.

Wait a second! *I* wrote those words in a novel some fourteen years earlier, *Alone in Death*. They were spoken by one of my characters as he lay in the middle of some desolate battlefield. Shot and wounded, left to die, he considered his own end as something tragic and yet noble.

Didn't sell a single copy of that POS either. Thinking on it, I've written some great quotes that no one will ever know about. How funny is that? But again, digression.

I was even fuller of shit those many years ago. There's nothing noble about dying on a battlefield. You're just dying in some crappy field, shortly to become a putrid carcass that has to be removed by those who fought the good fight and survived. Not only survived but were victorious over their fears and weaknesses. And there it was for me to see. True nobility lies not in dying as a vanquished victim in some senseless battle, but in avoiding the battle altogether. But if all else fails and there is a battle, I would rather be ignobly alive than nobly dead. If alive, perhaps some nobility could be restored after a time, even to a mashmeister like me. If dead, you rot. I wonder, do dead alcoholics rot or cure?

But now new words filled my heart, along with new meaning. Regardless of what we carry within us, that being either ignobility or nobility, we are never given more than what we have prepared ourselves to receive.

I saw it clearly now. I'm an author. I write for my living. I was prepared to handle this situation. If I had indeed created these circumstances, then I was more than capable of changing them. I was more than capable of rising above them and finding the solution.

Jack. My beloved Jack sat staring back at me. That glorious black label challenged me to become great. That chestnut brown liquid yearned to be one with me in becoming more than I ever thought I could be. So I yielded to its call and drank about a quarter of the bottle.

I stood up from the log I had perched upon ten minutes earlier and, staggering around the small opening, I gathered all of my courage. I summoned the greatness that I knew existed within the marrow of my being.

This demon nemesis, this horrid evil thing that seemed to possess me, *The Story*, was created so that I might do battle against it, so that I might see myself rise to its challenge with resolve and bravery and a sense of enduring. I saw the nobility of it all.

I took another long swallow of golden brown reality and all those ridiculous notions of courage, nobility, and challenge left me. Whew, I thought, those stupid thoughts almost found a home in an empty dwelling.

Here was the true bite of reality: I wasn't prepared to fight anyone or anything. I was an author looking to find my way back to literary relevance. Or, more to the truth of it, I was an alcoholic looking for another drink.

In my view, when the going gets tough, the smart get going. And I was going to get the hell outa Dodge right now. Like a scared kitten, I was going meow my ass out of here before The Story sent another character in place of the ninja chick, one that was even more provocative and professional — and more deadly.

I took another long swallow. I snickered. The thought of me being some kind of noble hero seemed so very absurd. What bullshit was I capable of believing unchecked? I took another drink to kill off any other stray hints of ridiculous nobility.

* * * * *

I checked my watch. It read 3:42. I was impressed that I had lasted as long as I had out here in the frosty elements. I chuckled about it.

I chuckled too soon.

I heard the hiss in the darkness and felt the arrow slice through my left shoulder and stop. It happened so fast, I hardly felt it when it struck. But that didn't last long.

I cringed. I bellowed. I took off like a gazelle.

I ran for another twenty minutes or so, until the pain in my shoulder crumpled me to my knees.

I heard her call out from afar.

"Are you still with me, Vincent?"

I didn't reply. I gathered my strength, stood up, and kept running, thinking all the time, stick the nobility of a good fight where the sun don't shine. I just wanted to get the hell outa the line of fire.

Just then I burst through the trees and found myself in the clearing that I knew was there.

Minutes later I was hidden away on the opposite side of the clearing with a clear line of sight, such it was in the dark, across the meadow to the other side.

A lake on the left and a stone cliff on the right naturally formed a gauntlet.

In the summer it was a beautiful meadow with sweetly aromatic wildflowers growing everywhere. It was a splendid place to come and sit and be at one with glorious nature.

For now, however, it provided the perfect killing zone. If she pursued me, she'd have to come through the meadow. If she did that, I'd blow her head off. How's that for nobility?

What strange thoughts fill the mind of one so pickled. I just had to chuckle softly once again.

I discovered a nice log. I sat down, and for the first time I had the chance to examine my wound. Sure enough, the arrow was sticking out of my shoulder, both front and back.

I reached up to it, thinking I'd break it off and pull it out of my shoulder, but then I thought about it again. It might be better to leave it where it was for the time being. It sealed the wound and controlled the bleeding. In fact, it wasn't bleeding all that much. If I removed it, I'd run a greater risk of bleeding out or of it getting infected. Then I noticed a detail. The damn thing was metal, not wood. I had nothing that would break the shaft anyway.

I heard her again. From the lack of volume, I guessed she was still a ways away — she hadn't gotten to the clearing yet.

"You gotta be in a lot of pain, Vincent. Me too. You put a bullet straight through my shoulder. It hurts like hell right now. Let's call it even-steven and go back to the house. You can finish the story and this all can end."

I had food, water, ammunition, and one more bottle of Jack. I was determined to see it through or find a way out of here.

My shoulder hurt, no doubt about it, but I sure as hell wasn't going to take the word of an assassin that all would be forgiven if I gave up. I may have looked stupid, but I could prove it.

What the hell did I mean by that?

Okay. I admit that didn't come off sounding the way I intended it to sound. The point is, I wasn't stupid enough to think that The Story would let me off the hook this late in the game. If it was still hunting me, it meant to finish me off.

I saw this as a battle I needed to win. I needed to put this ninja down and then I needed to get back to my house, get some things together, and make a run for it before the deputies showed up looking for blood.

My eyes searched through the rifle scope for any sign of my huntress. I saw nothing.

Then she called out to me again.

"Come on, Vincent. Let's end this."

She sounded like she was just on the other side of the clearing now, heading straight at me. If I could hold out just a while longer and not surrender to the pain in my shoulder, I might have the edge I needed.

I removed my pack with great care to not hit the arrow and cause me to cry out in pain. I got hold of my last bottle of Jack Daniel's and opened it. I drank several swallows and then got the bright idea to pour it over my wounds. That was soon deemed to be a big mistake.

I poured it over my shoulder. I shuddered from the pain. I held my voice. I got woozy. I swayed back and forth. I think I would have passed out completely if the ninja hadn't called out again.

"Vincent! It'll be daylight soon. You won't have the cover of darkness to hide behind much longer. I don't want this anymore. Let's go finish the story."

I fought off the pain and regained my wits. I peered through the scope. I saw a flash of light — a reflection of some kind. I had her in the crosshairs. I tried to use my left hand to steady the rifle, but I couldn't raise my arm without cringing.

I held the rifle the best I could with one arm. It was shaky as hell. I then dropped down next to the log and used that to support the rifle. It worked. It wasn't by any means perfect, but it steadied it enough to sight in on her.

As I'd expected, she stepped out into the clearing and stopped. The sudden presence of the clearing surprised her. It was exactly what I needed.

I aimed and fired.

She went down hard.

I worked the bolt, reloading the chamber, and then reacquired her in the scope and watched to see if she bounded up again like before. She didn't. What I could see of her was down. She stayed down.

I wanted to jump up and yell, but my shoulder kept me quiet and still. I began sweating from the pain that was beginning to build strongly.

After staring at her body for several more minutes and not seeing it move, I figured I had triumphed. Now to get home.

To get out of the area and avoid getting too close to her, just in case she was playing possum or was just unconscious, I decided to move down toward the lake and follow the shoreline around to the other side of the clearing and then skedaddle on down the mountain.

I tried to put on my backpack again, but I couldn't stand the pain. No matter how much Jack I drank, the pain would not subside. I'd have to leave the pack. I had no choice.

If she was dead, then it didn't matter anyway. If she was hit but alive, she wasn't going to come after me without doing more damage to herself.

I dropped the pack to the ground and walked away. I had my rifle and my bottle of Jack to carry, but I realized I couldn't carry both at the same time. I couldn't get any strength in my left hand to hold anything of any weight. That included the Jack bottle.

I grabbed a handful of cartridges from the pack and stuffed them into my jacket's right front pocket. I slung my rifle over my right shoulder and put a death grip on Jack's neck with my right hand.

"Let's get the hell outa here, Jack," I murmured.

CHAPTER 19

Moving as quietly as possible, it took me about fifteen minutes to negotiate around the lake edge and the clearing before I was walking on the path down the mountain toward my house.

With any luck, I would get back home around sunup. My shoulder pain was getting worse, and I didn't know how long I could hold out. I worried about passing out and being discovered. But I kept walking. I kept believing that I could get back alive. The words returned to my mind: *Fools believe like no others*.

Along the way, to keep my mind occupied and not thinking about the pain, I played over and over the ninja's words to me throughout this ordeal.

She, The Story, whatever, was really insistent that I finish the story. If I did, she'd asserted, then all of this would end. I considered what she said while huffing and puffing down the road, never certain just what she meant by it except that I might just have to get back to the house and write the damn story to its conclusion for no other reason than to end this nightmare once and for all. If that indeed would end it.

As for the next story, I'd worry about that some other time. Or maybe I would have to give up writing altogether. I was going to keep all my options open.

* * * * *

I could see a suggestion of morning light on the eastern horizon. Sunrise was a short time away, and with the hint of sunlight, I was beginning to think that I had weathered the worst of it.

My shoulder was hurting and I had drunk the last of Jack a while ago. Any additional pain was going to have to be endured without Brother Jack's help. Any newfound courage would necessarily have to come from my inner being instead. I thought about that. Shit! I'm a dead man.

I began to recognize my surroundings. I was about a mile from home. I was gaining confidence.

Then I saw a pair of headlights pop over the dip in the road. It was too late. The lights struck me. I ran off the road and back into the trees. The vehicle stopped.

Two deputies jumped out of the vehicle.

"Stop! Sheriff's deputies! Stop! Stop or we'll fire!" They fired. They missed. They fired again. They missed cleanly.

The pain of pounding along through the forest brought tears to my eyes. I was crying like a baby, but I was running like a deer.

A stump jumped up out of the darkness and caught me. I spilled over it and to the ground. I sat up and immediately brought my rifle up onto the stump. One of the deputies filled my scope. I fired. He dropped dead.

The other stopped his pursuit and hid behind a tree as I tried to work the bolt using one hand as before. This time, however, it wasn't going so well.

"Vincent Hobbs!" he yelled. "You're under arrest. Drop your weapon and come out with your hands high. This is your one and only warning."

I was in such pain, my mind snapped.

I sang my reply. "I shot the deputies, but I did not shoot the sheriff," changing around the lyrics of the famous Bob Marley song.

I heard a hiss. I heard a thud. The deputy stepped out from behind the tree, an arrow through his neck. He staggered a few steps, then dropped to the ground.

"You owe me, Vincent!" shouted a familiar voice.

Oh, Christ! The ninja was still alive.

I didn't answer. Instead, I stood up and started trotting toward my house. My mind was not functioning at full capacity. I was a wounded animal operating on instinct alone.

"I see you, Vincent. Stop running."

I didn't stop running.

I heard the familiar hiss. A second later, an arrow sliced through my lower left thigh. Just like the shoulder, I didn't feel the full pain immediately. I kept running.

Seconds later, I looked down and saw the arrowhead sticking out of the front of my thigh. I nearly fainted. But instead I discovered some miniscule amount of courage and resolve still living a life within me. I turn to see the ninja about seventy-five yards away, nocking her next arrow.

I fought through the horrendous pain and lifted my rifle using both hands, aimed quickly, and found her in my scope just as she raised the bow to aim. I fired. Miracles do happen occasionally. She was hit and again fell down. Once again, though, I couldn't tell if it was a fatal shot or not. Maybe there is no such thing as a fatal shot for fictional characters. As many times as Wile E. Coyote falls off a cliff or gets run over by a truck, he never dies. What if it's the same for this ninja? I thought. Oh, Christ! I wished I had my bottle of Jack at that moment.

I hobbled away, now in great pain, hoping I'd be able to kill off this ninja somehow.

That last mile was going to take forever at this rate, but I fought through the pain to keep walking. I wasn't about to quit now that I was so close.

The rifle was much too heavy for me now. I barely had the strength left to walk, let alone carry a rifle. Reluctantly, I let it slip from my hands to the ground and walked away from it.

I heard her scream. She was not dead. I was doomed, but I kept walking, refusing to give up.

"Vincent!" she hollered. "End this."

I didn't know if she was asking me to go back and end her life or get back to the house and write the story. I ignored her and kept walking, in too much pain to think clearly.

"Vincent!" she called out again.

I turned to see her silhouette against the lightening sky. She stumbled after me, falling and rising and falling again. She was still fifty yards away and not able to walk any faster than I could, apparently.

My bullets had struck her as hard as her arrows had struck me. We were both substantially incapacitated and virtually incapable of extending this fight much longer.

"Vincent!" she shouted again. "End me, please. I can't exist like this."

I finally gathered myself and turned toward her while walking backward, away from her. "I don't know how to end your pain. I don't know how to end my own."

"Finish me."

"I can't."

I turned back toward my house and continued walking, if dragging my left foot along behind me could be called walking.

I looked over my shoulder and saw her rise up and walk a few yards before collapsing again to the dirt road.

We continued on like this for some time. As the sky continued to brighten, I saw her more clearly every minute.

There was no doubt about it. We had both sustained serious injuries that forbade any notion of a clean victory by either one of us.

She kept insisting that I finish her, but I was only interested in getting back to my house alive. She could do as she pleased. I didn't care anymore. Her needs were irrelevant. I suddenly felt like a turd.

I had written another story several years before, entitled *The End of Me*. It was a story about a man and woman on the outs in their relationship. I sold one copy.

The woman, Keri, was chastising her soon-to-be ex-lover — her soon-to-be-*dead* ex-lover.

With tears streaming down her face, she said, "The cruelest thing you can do to anyone is make them feel irrelevant. And that's what you did to me." Then she pulled the trigger.

There I was, hobbling through a forest, being pursued by a fictional crazy ninja assassin, staring into the blackness that was my life at that moment, and feeling like shit because I had made The Story feel irrelevant by refusing to finish it.

God, how I missed Brother Jack.

CHAPTER 20

Another obscure portion of the letter from René Le Chant, written to his longtime companion, Mademoiselle Simone Chevalier, came back to me as I hobbled toward my house, still slightly ahead of my pursuing ninja.

"Its eyes closed. The tears slipped from between the lashes, slid down its face, and finally fell into oblivion off its chin. Its voice quieted. Its heart fell silent. Its life was over. It was time to rest. The story was told. It was now —"

I heard a twig snap.

I stopped and froze. I looked about everywhere. There was no sign of Regina. I stepped again. A twig snapped. Goddamn it! It was me.

I squatted down and remained still. Thoughts of Le Chant's letter to his companion returned.

I'd never figured out why he had written those lines or why he used the pronoun he did until that moment. Everything he'd done now made sense to me.

It became so very clear to me. I had to make it back home and finish the story or I would never again know peace. I would end up destroyed like Le Chant. "To hell with that," I said with resolve. To hell with everything and everyone else.

What a coldhearted bastard I was, but my task was clear now. I felt zero compassion.

Just then I stumbled and fell to the ground. I was in too much pain to rise to my feet, so I crawled, making my way through the thistles and sharp vines of the undergrowth. The arrows in my leg and shoulder left me in horrendous pain. To even touch them caused great agony.

Still, I had to hide and slide my way through the forest, my only thought getting back to my house in time to end all of this. I repeated my purpose over and over in my head. I had developed a great plan to end this horror. I had only to survive long enough to get back to my house and implement it.

I heard her stalking me. She was unabashed in her tracking of me. She knew I had nothing to defend myself with. I think she was enjoying herself.

I could almost feel her eyes searching for me. Hell, I could almost feel the heat of their stare upon my back.

"Vincent," she called out. "Come on, Vincent. I still want to play."

She didn't want to play, but she didn't want me to know it straight out.

Of course, I stayed as quiet as a dead branch. But I had to get back to my house. That was all I could concentrate on doing. I heard her stomping through the brush several yards away and then falling with a thud to the ground. From the fading sound, it appeared that she was walking away from me. I waited until she was several yards farther away before I continued my painful crawl back toward my house, wondering why she was suddenly walking away from me.

"Vincent, my little pincushion, I know you're out here," I heard her call out. Her voice now told me that she was at least fifty yards away, but I couldn't tell if she was walking toward me again or away from me. I heard her body hit the ground once more. She must have hit hard for me to hear it this far away.

This was insane. I had to make the effort and rise up. Hobbling along would be much faster than crawling. I neared a tree and used it to help me to my feet. My leg wound was now bleeding badly, but not so much that I feared bleeding out before I could get back to my house.

Rising up onto my feet was painful as hell. Several times I almost shouted out from the agony, but barely managed to restrain myself. Any shout would undoubtedly give away my position. The last thing I wanted was another arrow in me.

I got my legs moving, but the pain nearly caused me to fall back to the ground many times. Still, every step I took in the direction of my house was another step farther away from Regina Pepper, ninja assassin. Damn, I thought, The Story is for shit at naming its characters. But why was I thinking about that? I wondered. Oh yeah, anything to keep my mind off the pain. I sure needed Jack back.

My house was now only about 200 feet from where I stood. I calculated in my head that I'd reach it within ten to fifteen minutes at the rate I was hobbling along. Probably closer to fifteen if I had to stop and rest.

That was, of course, highly dependent on Regina not discovering her error and turning back toward me. To put it bluntly, though, it didn't look good for me.

I began thinking that I should have put more effort into the original story. I mean, a guy going into a bar and meeting this dynamite-looking psycho bitch killer *does* have certain elements of intrigue and guile in and of itself. I could have done something fun with it before all the blood and brain splatter. Indeed, it would have been much easier than trudging through the forest at night with two arrows stuck in me.

Regina wasn't wrong. I felt like a pincushion.

What was I thinking taking on a ninja assassin created by some demon story? I love Jack, but I was beginning to think that Jack Daniel's was an inestimable part of this whole tragedy.

I had to stop thinking about drinking. I was about to go ape shit without the stabilizing effects of feeling a bottle in my hand and a warm splash of Jack in my belly. In fact, it had been how long since I'd last taken a drink? I didn't know, but I was damn near sober as a judge, although I've seen some judges pretty blasted in my time.

And they're sneaky little bastards about it, too. Always in the darkest part of the bar, trying to stay out of the limelight, living in fear that they might be discovered by someone they gave a stiff sentence to for doing exactly what they're doing themselves at that moment.

Damn judges! Damn agents! Damn publishers! Damn computers! Damn ninjas! Damn story!

I heard Regina call out for me again. To my great delight she was even farther away now, still heading in the wrong direction. I had a bit of a chuckle thinking that this crazy-ass ninja assassin chick wasn't the sharpest pencil in the box after all. If I remained lucky, I'd get back to my house before she realized her error and caught up with me. I really did feel bad for what I had put her through, but she was trying to kill me, so all bets were off.

Dear God! A knowing thought then hit me.

The complete answer to my problem came clearly to me. Why hadn't I thought of it before? I knew how to end the madness. I think Regina knew it, too, but she didn't know how to tell me. I had a plan after all. I only needed to get back to my house in time to put my plan into action.

I farted.

All was right with the world once again.

Despite all of this embarrassing but natural release of gas, I could find no fault with Mister Jack Daniel's, *mon ami de confiance* (my trusted friend). It's just the nature of Jack, and anyone who drinks it regularly knows this. Or it was, at the very least, my own personal reaction to the extended imbibing of the nectar. Of course, I don't know many drunks who are farting while running for their very lives. *Stop!* my mind screamed. *This isn't funny at all!*

I stopped thinking about farts the moment I came over the rise and saw my house lit up like a rock concert.

I never knew Park County had that many sheriff's deputies.

Easing toward my house, I could see the many sheriff's cars parked out front. As I had figured, they were waiting for me. No doubt The Story had warned them of my possible return. They weren't being very stealthy about it, but it didn't matter. Into that house I had to get if I was to end this nightmare.

I then remembered the broken glass in my basement window. The only real difficulty in achieving my entrance to the basement was the fact that I had to lower myself into the well without alerting the deputies.

I glanced down at my leg. Jesus Christ, I thought, I'm going to have to Lonesome Dove these arrows. For those of you unacquainted with that term, I meant that I'd have to break off the feathered end and push the arrows through my legs and shoulder. It was going to hurt like hell. There was no getting around that fact. I decided to make it happen while I was still out in the woods.

Christ! They were metal. How did I forget that small detail? Then I remembered my pocketknife. I pulled it out and opened it. My plan was simple. I'd slice off the feathers and then pull the arrow through my leg. Yeah, I thought, it was a stupid plan, but I had no other choice, it seemed.

Still, I would have to hold my screams no matter the pain. One shout and the deputies would be on me within seconds, forever eliminating any chance I might have to resolve this whole terrifying experience.

I steadied myself and decided to go for the shoulder first. I reached back over my shoulder with the knife and sliced off the feathers, silently sobbing from the pain. Completing that, I grabbed the arrow shaft just above the arrowhead. I gritted my teeth and counted to three. Knowing that there was no avoiding the pain, my tears flowed like a waterfall, but they flowed silently.

The next part of the campaign to rid myself of the arrows was the toughest. I stiffened my hold on the arrow and gritted my teeth once again. I counted to three again. I did nothing. I counted to six. I was still afraid to pull the arrow shaft from my body. I counted to nine and yanked. The arrow shaft slipped right out, but not without nearly causing me to pass out. It hurt like nothing I had ever experienced before.

I looked at the wound, but in the fading moonlight the blood looked black. To my amazement, there wasn't much of it.

Next came the arrow through my thigh. I sliced off the feathers as before. The shock of pulling the arrow from my body was over. I knew pulling it through my leg was going to be equally painful, but I was prepared for the pain this time. I didn't count at all. I just tugged the arrow out of my leg with one swift move. Hurt it did, but not as much as my shoulder had. I marveled at how I had handled the arrows' extraction so well.

I had gone with the pain. I had allowed it to be what it needed to be. But I had persevered through it and now it was subsiding quickly, so I could turn my attention to crawling down into the window well and slipping into the basement. Hopefully, there would be no deputy in the basement — or in the house, for that matter.

I would have to move quickly and silently upstairs to my computer and resolve this nightmare once and for all. I just hoped no one had moved my computer and that it was still on.

I moved as I had planned, quickly and silently over to the window well. Although the pain of pulling the arrows out of my body had diminished, the pain of the wounds was still agonizing, but I was controlling the degree to which I would allow it to hinder my efforts. And to that end, I refused to yield to it.

I dropped into the well easily and squatted to see if there might be a deputy in the basement waiting to ambush me. There was no one in there that I could see. So I crawled through the window and lowered myself to the concrete floor. Phase one was complete. I was in.

Now I had to get up the stairs without getting caught. I moved toward the stairs. That's when I heard voices coming from the upper floors. Some of the deputies were definitely inside the house.

I took a moment to think. Meanwhile, I grabbed some pieces of clean laundry and wrapped my wounds as best as I could.

I heard doors opening and closing. The deputies were going in and out of my house. I had no idea how many were there, but even one was too many. I didn't have the strength to fight, but I knew I had to get to the computer or it was all over for me. The ninja bitch would return to the house very soon, if she wasn't already on her way.

I heard the front door open again and then shut. I did not hear any more voices. Had they all gone outside? Would they return anytime soon?

I realized that I might only have seconds at the computer. I hobbled over to the door to the garage and locked it. If someone came into the house while I was on the stairs, it would only be through the front door.

I stood at the bottom of the stairway looking up toward the kitchen. One flight of stairs was all that separated me from the computer, but once I was in the middle of the stairs, there would be nowhere to hide if someone was up there and came to investigate any sound I might make while ascending. Once on the stairs, it was do or die.

I took the first step, and then the second. My leg was hurting so bad, I didn't think I could endure the pain for too much longer. This was a time when I could have really used some Jack to deaden the pain.

But I had none. I had to put both Jack and the pain out of my mind. I had to make it to the computer or my life was over.

I lifted my right foot onto the next stair and froze in fear. I heard someone get up from a chair somewhere in the kitchen area. I heard their footsteps. They were light steps, like that of a woman. I knew several of the deputies were women and so I reasoned that one of them was in my house. I suspected her to be keeping a vigil in case I returned. Well, here I was.

Then it hit me. A fart had been cooking in my belly for the last several minutes. It was ready to make an entrance into the world.

Under normal conditions I'd be howling with laughter at the thought of trying to sneak around while making like a foghorn. It was funny, I admit it. Farts are usually funny. But it wasn't funny at that particular moment. It was working out to be another huge Jack fart. I could feel the gas expanding in my gut and working its way toward my sphincter. Jesus, I thought, this felt like it was going to be a record setter.

I knew it was not going to come out gentle and silent. No, this was going to be what I call an ass ripper. One thing I'll say for Jack, he doesn't mess around with the little things. Everything Jack does, he does big. A big drunk. A big hangover. A big laugh. And, when it happens, a big fart.

I cringed with a gas pain. The fart wanted its liberty, and it was quickly working its way through the tunnel of freedom.

I heard the footsteps make their way toward the front door and then heard the door open and close. A question had to be answered before I could take another step. Did she leave or did she just open the door and then close it again?

I waited for any sound, but the sound most on my mind at that moment was the fart battling for its independence. If I didn't manage to release the gas delicately, I'd alert her to my presence in a very rude way. I could just see her entering the incident in her report: "I was alerted to the subject's location by way of a huge Jack fart."

I heard nothing upstairs. There were no footsteps coming back to the kitchen from the front door. I wasn't certain that she had left. Perhaps she was standing at the door looking out through the glass. I had no way to know for sure except to stay still and silent for a while longer, but then the thought came to me that perhaps she did go outside and would return very soon.

I had to get to the computer. I had to release a huge fart. I decided to do both at the same time.

A vision of Wile E. Coyote entered my brain. Wile E. has to run down the Road Runner on roller skates, so he farts, launching himself down the highway. Of course he doesn't quite have enough momentum to catch the Road Runner and stalls out in an intersection, where a huge tractor-trailer runs his ass over.

Funny to watch; not so funny for me, however. Well, it was … oh, never mind.

It was more than I could bear. The fart was coming, like it or not. I prepared to lift my foot onto the next stair knowing that as soon as did, I'd allow my sphincter to relax just enough to release the nuclear gas explosion.

The reality slapped me. My life had come down to whether or not anyone was up there to hear a fart. And I wasn't laughing about it.

I had to move. Time was running out fast. I decided I was going to go for it. I lifted my foot. BOOM!

I dashed up the stairway as fast as my arrow-aerated leg could carry me. I rounded the corner of the stairwell and saw no one there.

Good fortune and fools once more.

I raced to the computer, opened the lid, and pressed the space bar. Nothing happened. Someone had turned off my computer.

"No!" I muttered as I hit the 'on' switch.

My computer booted rather quickly; I didn't have a lot of programs on it to slow it down. Still, it would take a while to open the story document and bring this whole terrible experience to its justifiable end.

The computer booted up. Windows came alive.

Just then the front door opened. I looked up and directly into the eyes of the ninja assassin. She looked like shit, but she smiled at me.

"So you did make it back after all, Vincent. I'm so proud of you."

"How did you get back so fast?"

"The two deputies that we killed up in the forest? I drove the patrol car down. I knew you'd get back here."

I thought it a very clever move on her part. And here I'd thought she had lost her way earlier. Once more, fools and fortune.

Her hand flashed up and behind her. It suddenly held an arrow. She nocked it. "It's over for you, Vince. Come on in, boys. I am the master."

Just then two sheriff's deputies walked in, pointing their pistols at me. "You cop-killin' son of a bitch!" one of them shouted, his hate-filled eyes slicing through me.

My computer was ready. I hit the Word icon to start the program.

"No, *you're* the sons a bitches! I'm an author." I spat back at them, without looking up at her.

She pulled back the bowstring.

"I can end this for you," I said.

I clicked on the story document.

"Too late. I can finish it myself," she said.

"Have it your way."

The story came up.

"Bye-bye, Vinnie," she said.

She aimed the arrow at me.

I typed as she released the arrow.

I shut my eyes as I heard the hiss of the arrow taking flight. The deputies fired their guns.

And then there was silence.

Am I dead? I thought. Is this how death occurs?

I opened my eyes. The ninja was gone. The hissing arrow was gone. The deputies were gone. All the patrol cars with their flashing lights were gone. My wounds were gone. I was whole. I was sober. I was alone.

I looked down at the screen and smiled at the two words I had typed — the two words that had ended my nightmare. *The End.*

EPILOGUE

I sat on my couch waiting for a knock on the door.

It came.

I answered the door with a huge grin.

"Arnie! How are you?"

"Fine, my boy. Just fine."

"Come on in."

"Do you have it?"

"Right there on the table," I said, pointing to the computer table.

Arnie went straight to it and picked up the short stack of paper. He moved to the couch, collapsed onto it, and began reading without another word spoken.

I moved to the computer table and smiled. "Would you like a drink, Arnie? I only have juice, but it's pretty good."

"No, thanks, kid. I'm good. Leave me alone for a while, please. I'm dying to see what you've come up with."

"Sure thing, buddy."

Another knock on the door. It was Sheriff Dell Overly.

I opened the door.

"Howdy, Dell."

"Hi ya, Vince. How are you doing?"

"Just fine, Dell. Come on in."

Dell walked in and spotted Arnie. "Howdy, Mister Feinstein. How are you today?"

"Just fine, Sheriff Overly. I came up to read what Vincent has been working on the last month. He always waits until the last moment to do this, but he's never disappointed me yet."

He went back to reading.

"What brings you up here, Dell?" I asked.

"The battery charger. I told you I'd bring it up a few days ago. But things just sort of went crazy for me. Sorry about that. I set it in front of the garage door."

"Hey, thanks, Dell. I appreciate that very much. I'll let it charge up good and then I'll drop the charger back by your office."

"That'd be just fine, Vince. No rush."

"Can I offer you a glass of juice?"

"No, no, I've got to get back to the office. But I've got to tell you this, Vince. Sitting up here all alone like you do for so long, so far from civilization, if it were me, I'd drink myself drunk each day. This is too isolated for me up here."

"Carla's business trips do take her away for extended periods, but she intends to retire by the end of the year, so it'll get better soon. And good thing for me I never acquired the taste for alcohol. Besides, I've got other things to do with my brain cells."

"Well, that's a fine thing. We've got too many drunks on the road as it is. Did Carla get back from her trip yet?"

"Last night. She ran into Fairplay to do some grocery shopping. She should be home any minute now."

At that moment I spotted Carla's car drive into the yard.

"There she is right now."

"I'll say hello to her on my way out. Probably should move the battery charger before she opens the garage door and runs over it. Take care, Vincent."

"Thanks again, Dell. Say hello to all the guys and gals down at the office."

"Will do."

Dell left and I shut the door.

"I gotta go help Carla with the groceries, Arnie."

He didn't answer, just waved his hand at me.

I helped Carla carry all the groceries up the stairs and dropped the bags on the counter.

"Hi, Arnie," she said.

"Hello, my dear."

"He's reading, honey. Better we leave him alone for a while."

"He's gonna love it," she said. "But did I really have to turn into a werewolf? Was that really necessary?" She smiled and socked my arm playfully.

"Everybody got in on this one, sweetie."

"But a werewolf? Really?"

"It was a lot of fun. Go with it."

"I told Regina at the supermarket that she was a ninja assassin archer."

"Yeah? And?"

"She just laughed and said she could hardly wait to read about it."

"Bart Gamble?!" said Arnie without looking up from the page. "Jesus Christ, Vincent. I remember him. Yeah, *A Good Day for a Gunfight*. Your first Western. My God, kid. This is amazing. You really went into your bag of tricks on this one." He chuckled and then returned to reading.

* * * * *

Arnie picked up the stack of pages and stood up. He looked at me and grinned.

"Vincent, it's a number one best seller if I've ever seen one. You've got it all here, kid. Murder, mayhem, a werewolf, a ninja psycho killer, a lake full of bodies, exploding aliens, farts, and Jack Daniel's. I'm gonna have those publishers paying for this through the nose. Amazing work, my boy. The title is perfect, by the way. *The Story*. Absolutely amazing. And you nailed the drunk parts. How the hell you did that, I'll never know. I've never even seen you drink a beer. Damned amazing, kid."

"Are you sure you can't stay for dinner or a chat, Arnie?"

"Thank you, but no. I want to get this copied and out to the publishers first thing tomorrow morning. I can't wait to see the looks on their faces as I'm pitching this to them."

"Okay. We'll walk you out to your car."

"No need. I'll call you as soon as I know something."

Carla and I walked out onto the deck and stopped at the railing as Arnie skipped down the steps and to his car. He stopped before opening the door and looked up at me and smiled. "A guy walks into a bar!" he shouted, then shook his head and climbed into his car. I nodded, smiling.

We sat waving at him as his car drove away and then we walked back into the house. I went over to the fireplace to start a fire as Carla headed for the kitchen. As I turned on the gas I noticed the silver candelabra was crooked and straightened it out.

Carla screamed. I turned quickly to see her looking at the computer.

"What is it?" I asked.

Staring blankly, she didn't or couldn't answer me. She pointed at the computer.

I walked over to see what all the commotion was about. On the screen were five sentences.

"ARNIE FEINSTEIN STOPPED NEXT TO HIS CAR AND THEN GLANCED BACK UP AT HIS FRIEND AND CLIENT, THE RICH AUTHOR. HE HATED HIM FOR HIS TALENT, HIS SKILL, HIS PRESTIGE, HIS FAME. "A GUY WALKS INTO A BAR!" HE SHOUTED. THEN HE SMILED THROUGH JEALOUS EYES, KNOWING

**AT THAT VERY MOMENT EXACTLY
HOW HE WAS GOING TO MURDER
VINCENT HOBBS. I AM THE MASTER."**

The End

About the Author

Val Edward Simone was born in Seattle, Washington, and has been writing since 1980.

Val has published adult-themed action/adventure novels; historical fiction; western novels; short stories; a collection of thoughts, musings, and observations; a collection of children's short stories; and several children's picture books. He continues to work on many other novels, short stories and screenplays.

He is also a strong advocate of early childhood development through the arts, and continues to support all efforts toward helping children discover their own creativity through reading, writing, and drawing.

Val currently lives and writes in Arizona.

His websites:
EkidslandPublishing.com
MorningsidePublishing.com
Ekidsland.com (For kids only)

Connect with Val and Other Books

Twitter: @valsimone
Instagram: @valedwardsimone

Other Books by Val Edward Simone
Novels/Novellas
Blood Trackers: One Crazy Love Story
Blood Trackers 2: Revenge of an Angel
About Things I Lost Long Ago…scribblings from a foolish heart
The Wondrous Life of a Long-Ago Man
Comes the Devil to Crooked Creek
Captain Delightable's Magical Tales of a Minchon Warrior
A Minute of Forever
Into the Light Boldly…an odyssey of self-discovery
The Firestone…Is Mankind Ready?
The Story
Adventures at Dead River
The Art of Living Between Hell and Breakfast
5th Avenue Whore

Short Stories
Manifest Destiny
The Secret Life of Gonner Andling
Love Bytes
Dragons Within
The Problem with Dragons
The Unfortunate Dragon
The Fairy Collection
Through the Waterfall
Fairy Forgotten
Emily's Wish
Kaylee's Secret
The Wizard of Sebastianville

Children's Picture Books
Felix
The Gingerbread Pony
The Littlest Bell
Mean Muley McGrudge
Otto and Kevin
Proton Gator
Sammy Sparrow Spy

Children's Coloring Book
Proton Gator & Friends Coloring Book